IMMORTAL ......

THE TEARS OF LILITH

By Candace L. Bowser

ISBN: 978-1-257-86090-6

Prelude

Lilith stood upon the great mountain Atlen as she looked down upon those who served her. For a thousand years she had endured the cruel treatment of Enlil after he had created the bounty that lay below her. Her rage grew as Lilith gazed angrily at those he loved above all others, those he adored more than his own kind. The humans had taken precedence in the life of the one Lilith had loved more than life itself. Enlil had turned away from not only Lilith but all who resided within the Hall of the Gods. Tears streamed down her face as the Gods plotted against him. The War in Heaven had begun, an Immortal War that would end with no victors and no champions; only an unleashed darkness over which Lilith would have no control.

Dedication

Every writing endeavor has one person behind the scenes whose encouragement inspires the pursuit. This book is dedicated to Kelli Gresham for all the countless times she encouraged me to continue my work on this novel and for her undying support of all my printed works. Thank you for your friendship.

Table of Contents

Chapter One
The War in Heaven

The soft breeze of summer blew across the fields causing the tall grass to sway gently. The world below her had only been formed for two days, yet it was breathtakingly beautiful. Lilith looked down on the creation of her beloved Enlil and wept over its beauty.

Her tears were not only for the beauty of the world he had created beneath her; but also for the world they had lost. Lilith's heart was heavy with the memories of their homeland and those who had perished there. She wondered in silence if the other Gods felt the same as she did. Had they dabbled in the nature of things they should have left alone? Now their home was uninhabitable, a virtual wasteland, and had become a desolate, fiery, red planet which was crumbling.

The deaths were so senseless, without meaning. They darkened her ability to remain optimistic for what laid ahead of them. Lilith had once pleaded with Enlil to not create the tiny creatures he desired. She told him what he asked of her was dangerous, that they would not be able to withstand the gift that she alone could give them. Enlil became obsessed with his current whim and Lilith's words were like the wind to him.

Over the next several days, Enlil created the animals over which Enlil would give Lilith reign and it pleased her. She watched the many creatures that now roamed her lover's newly created world and rejoiced. The animals were varied and completed each other. Predator and prey coexisted peacefully without malice. Perhaps they could live here and be happy. Perhaps they would not repeat the mistakes of their past.

The original home of the Gods was very similar to the one Enlil had created on Earth. All manners of wondrous beasts had roamed freely. Ice glistened on the mountain on which the Gods dwelled and rivers flowed in the valleys below them. The soft and lush world they came to love flourished under the care of Lilith. In her happiness, flowers grew beneath her feet as she walked through the valley of the home he created for her. Enlil was so pleased at Lilith's happiness he erected a magnificent temple in Lilith's honor. It was a Ziggurat which had an elaborately carved relief of her face so that he could behold her beauty. He had told Lilith it was so he could see her effigy from Heaven. That was now all in the past. Her temple lied in ruins, barely recognizable to those who did not know what it was. All that remained of her beautiful temple was the shadowy outline of face in the red desert sand.

Enlil grieved for the humans who had perished in their former homeland. His grief was so deep he retreated from the other Gods. He no longer showed Lilith the affection he once had. She grew lonely in his long absences. Her heart longed for love and to be loved the same as any other woman. Enlil was the most beautiful of all the Gods in Lilith's eyes. She desired him and him alone. Enlil's father, the great sky-god An, disappeared into the primeval darkness when his son had killed all that he had created on their former homeland. Many centuries would pass before An would be seen again.

Enlil was sometimes cruel to Lilith. When he decided he wanted to have a child to stand at his side and help him to rule his new race of beings, he did not choose Lilith to be his consort. When Enlil's throne bearer and sacred attendant learned about Enlil's plan to create the nighttime sky and have a son with Ninlil, it was Ennugi who took Lilith away to prevent her destructive rage. Lilith was so distraught over the union of her only love with another Goddess she unleashed her rage upon any God within her path. Lilith had helped Enlil to separate Heaven from Earth so that the Heavens could be formed. As the first Goddess, the Goddess born of primeval darkness, it was her right to become Enlil's wife. Ennugi knew Lilith would become filled with rage at hearing the news and feared for the other Gods, so he took her to the Great Mountain Atlen on the newly formed land beneath them. Ennugi knew Lilith's temper was formidable and vengeful, but she was also quick to grant forgiveness.

While Lilith contemplated her place in the new world Enlil had created, Ninlil gave birth to a beautiful son whom they named Nanna. Eventually Lilith came to love him as though he were her own child and lavished him with many gifts including creating the moon that now graced the night sky of their new home. Each night as she lay in the cool grass of the mountain, Lilith would gaze upon the beauty of the moon above her. The beauty of the luminous sphere gave her a sense of peace that she had not known in many years

Enlil had a fondness for the humans he had once created that lived on the planet they called their home so long ago. The more obsessed he became with creating humans on their new home, the less attention he paid to Lilith. She could not understand his fascination with these tiny creatures he created in his own image. They were small and insignificant compared to the Gods. For some reason that Lilith could not understand, they made Enlil happy. Therefore, Lilith consented to his whim and said nothing when he announced to the other Gods that he wished to create the same human race on Earth. Perhaps if she supported him in his creation of these tiny creatures, he could once again love her.

The other Gods did not agree with Enlil's decision to re-create the humans and soon the Gods were divided. Inanna, Enlil's granddaughter, was quick to take his side in the battle over the humans. Inanna was going to be given a new title, and she was not about to allow the other Gods to take it away from her. For nearly a millennia she had been the Goddess of War, creating havoc in the Heaven's, but Enlil now wished her to become a mother Goddess to his race of humans. It was not a title she was willing to let slip through her fingers.

Inanna was as beautiful as the sun and her wings were as strong and graceful as any eagle. Her long flowing white gowns reminded Lilith of the moon which she had created for her father, Nanna, so many years ago. The trait that Lilith had admired about Inanna the most, her fierce warrior aspect, was now what she was eagerly willing to abandon in order to serve the humans. However, not all the Gods were so pleased with Enlil's latest endeavor, and they conspired against him; including Ninlil and Enlil's second born son Nergal.

Nergal and Lilith were very close. She admired his strength and masculinity. His muscular physique was perfect. He wielded a double-edged mace-scimitar which was embellished with lions to honor Lilith. Lions were among Lilith's favorite creatures on their new home planet; it was Nergal's way of showing his appreciation toward her. Nergal had never agreed with the way Enlil toyed with Lilith's affections. He knew how deep Lilith's love for his father ran and did not approve of how he used Lilith for his own personal motives. For his loyalty to her, Lilith granted Nergal the power over sudden death, plagues, and made him the Ruler of the Underworld. Nergal was the first to stand against Enlil as the War of the Immortals began.

Nergal desperately desired Lilith to side with him, as the battle was set into motion. He wanted Lilith to be free of the hold his father had over her and for Lilith to be a Goddess of her freewill so that she might find love.

"I cannot betray the love I have for your father. I will not stand against Enlil," Lilith said firmly as Nergal approached her.

"I cannot understand why you support him when he has done nothing but cause you pain. You have loved him above all others and forsaken your own happiness just to be near him. He holds the humans in higher regard than he does his own kind and his own children!" Nergal said angrily.

"I cannot go against the one I love, and until he gives me reason to not support him, I shall remain neutral. I cannot take sides in this war Nergal, no matter how much it pains me to be unable to stand with you. I love your father, and I cannot go against him," Lilith said as she touched Nergal's face and stroked his beard.

Nergal closed his eyes and nodded his head in reluctant acceptance though he could not understand Lilith's reasoning given how his father treated her. Lilith could soothe the heart of any God or human just by merely touching them. Nergal felt the depth of the love she had for his father in her touch and could not be angry with her.

"Please understand I must do what I feel in my heart is necessary. I only ask that you do not interfere as I approach the other Gods. I too must follow my heart Lilith," Nergal whispered as he backed away from Lilith and disappeared.

Nergal appealed to the other Gods to help him overthrow his father and stop him from making the same mistake he had before in the further creation of the human race. He called to Ningal and asked the River Goddess to weave a mist and enshroud the heavens so that the world below would not be able to see the war in heaven. Since Ningal was one of the many lovers of Nergal's brother Nanna, she agreed to help him with his quest. Ningal called upon Ningirama to aid her with his magic. Together they wove a golden mist that wove its way through the Heavens and obscured them from the few humans in existence below.

It pleased Nergal that his mother stood beside him as the war began. Ninlil too was angry with Enlil and his preferential treatment of the humans. Were the Gods not the most beautiful creatures to ever inhabit the Heavens? It struck Nergal as strange that his mother would agree with Lilith. It also puzzled him why Lilith would not stand against Enlil when even his mother agreed with him. She knew how deep the love for Enlil was within Lilith's heart. She had also seen the cruelty in his ways when he neared Lilith. Lilith was a strong Goddess; but when it came to Enlil she was weak. This angered Ninlil, not for the weakness Lilith had in her desire for love, but in the fact that Enlil abused Lilith's love for him.

Ninlil raised her arms and drew the golden mist to concel them. The chariots of the Gods rolled across the battlefield in front of Ninlil to prepare for war. In the sorrow Ninlil felt in her heart, she lowered her head and closed her eyes. Perhaps today his cruelty toward them would end.

For forty days, the Heavens were enshrouded in a dense, dark mist which hid the actions of Nergal as he gathered the Gods against his father. Nergal enlisted the aid of Mes An Du and Sara, Inanna's son, to help him defeat his father. When the end of forty days came, Nergal, Mes An Du, and Sara stood with over one hundred lesser Gods ready to make war against Enlil. Belet-Seri stood on the edge of the battlefield, her tablet readied to record those who fell so that they might be granted entrance into the Underworld.

When the mist lifted, the War of the Immortals began. Nergal, Mes An Du, and Sara stood against the minions of Enlil. Nergal twirled his battleax in his hands as the followers of Enlil approached. The first lessor God to attack Nergal was met with the swift strike of his ax. Sara smiled as the lessor God was cleaved in half by Nergal's mighty strike. Sara desired carnage above even life and desired to be the sole God to one day insight war among the humans when the time came. The sounds of battle roared across the Heavens. The class of steel was heard between the screams of the wounded. Lilith covered her ears and wept at sounds of fellow kinsmen dying.

Lilith descended to the Great Mountain Atlen and watched the battle unfold with tears in her eyes. Though she could be vengeful and spiteful, Lilith had more love in her heart than any of the other Gods combined. She prayed her one and only true love, Enlil, would not be killed in the battle. What Lilith did not know was it would be but one of many wars fought for the control of Heaven over the millennia.

The skies grew dark and the clash of armor was echoed across the Heavens above her. It rolled across the Heavens and made what the humans called thunder. They did not understand the sounds they heard were their Gods at war, or that the rain which fell were the tears of those who served the Gods as they cried in anguish. The clash of their weapons caused lightning to flash across the nighttime sky, illuminating the battlefields of the Gods as they fought.

Nergal led the battle against his father. Mes An Du, Sara, and Mes Lam Taea shone brilliantly behind Nergal, blinding the other Gods to conceal Nergal's identity. The mighty War God Erra joined them in battle unleashing a fury against Enlil and his followers.

Each day the thunder would stop, along with the rain and the lightning. The Gods would gather their wounded along with their dead from the battleground of the Heavens. There were times when months would pass before the War of the Immortals would begin again. Lilith watched the humans as they cowered and hid from the sound of the battle above them. They were such frail and superstitious creatures. The more she was near them, the harder it was for her to understand how Enlil could love them more than his own kind, more than his own children.

Again, the war began. Lilith ascended to the Heavens to watch the battle unfold first hand. Nergal and his supporters had suffered many casualties. Enlil re-animated the fallen and called them to him, which gave him an unfair advantage over Nergal and his warriors. Enlil now fought with an unstoppable army. An army of cursed lessor Gods called the Jhinn who he forced to do his will. Lilith did not feel the balance was fair nor could she believe that Enlil would do this to his own son. The mighty God Erra and the Sebitti along with Sara were not enough to give Nergal the advantage he needed as he fought against this father and his deceitful ways. Lilith stepped in front of Nergal as he cleaned his mace and pleaded with him.

"You cannot win this war. He uses his power to his advantage," Lilith said as she laid her hands upon Nergal's chest. She did not want Nergal to continue a battle she knew he could never win. Lilith knew in her heart it could be thousands of years before Nergal could gain ground against Enlil.

"Then give me the advantage that only you can give," Nergal replied as he dropped the mace from his hand.

"You do not know what you ask Nergal. To take from me is to take darkness into your heart. I cannot be responsible for what happens if you do so. You know what happened the last time I intervened. Our homeland fell to ruins, human turned against human, and mankind exterminated itself," Lilith whispered.

Lilith understood her place among the Gods. She was balance for without darkness there could be no light. Though Lilith was not completely dark in nature, and did possess light within her, it was not the core of her being. Lilith was the balance that kept the Heavens in their rightful place. She kept the balance between the Gods. It was her place to remain neutral and let freewill lead their fates. Lilith had interfered only once before at the insistence of another. It had resulted in the death of every single living being on their homeworld. She could not make that same mistake again. Her blood gave any immortal unparalleled strength along with many other dark gifts. Lilith was the only Goddess who possessed within her all the traits of every single God and Goddess within the Heavens, and that in itself was very dangerous. Lilith, the firstborn Goddess, was the purest source of vampire, the purest source of darkness, and the purest source of love.

Lilith watched the battle continue to unfold before her eyes. Enlil had lied to all of them. This new world they called their home was not for them to rebuild their lives as he had said. It was a place where he could put himself in the place of supreme ruler with the humans as his loyal and dedicated subjects. They would honor him not only as a King but also as their God. He would descend upon Sumeria and place his descendants as their Kings. He would give to them the sacred knowledge of the Well of Velspruga and allow them offences so that he could judge them. They, in turn, would offer him blood sacrifices and give their daughters and their wives to him without question. Moreover, what would Enlil give the humans in return? Nothing more than empty promises and broken dreams for Enlil would never bestow upon them the same powers which the Gods held. He reserved that power for himself alone.

Lilith thought of the many scenarios that could unfold with Enlil as the supreme ruler of an entire race who would bow at his feet. He had placed himself above her for the last time.

"If it is the power to defeat him with which you speak Nergal, I shall give this power to you," Lilith whispered.

She wrapped her arms firmly around Nergal's back and held him tightly. Lilith nearly swooned at his touch. It had been a thousand years since she had felt the embrace of another God, and it filled her soul with joy. Lilith laid her forehead against Nergal's massive and broad shoulder.

"Take from me my blood, and be the God of Destruction you were destined to be," she whispered.

Lilith pulled Nergal's dagger from its sheath and slid it across her shoulder. She eased his head forward until she could feel his breath hot against her skin. Only once before had she given her blood to another, and it was Enlil. She knew the consequences of her actions, yet she did not care. Lilith was the only Goddess who relied on the blood of others to sustain herself. She was the only God who refused to drink from the Velspruga, a sacred bowl which magically refilled itself with the nectar of the Gods each morning. Lilith survived and drew her power from her own choices. She could not take immortality from the Well just because it was her right as a Goddess.

As Nergal began to consume her blood, Lilith became filled with an overpowering desire to take his blood from him. Her sighs rang through the Heavens like the soft and enchanting sound of a harp as she parted her lips and her fangs slid forward. Enlil shuddered as her heard Lilith's enchanting song and knew she had found love in the arms of another. He also knew what this meant. Lilith had empowered another to stand against him with the same power that Lilith had once given to him.

As Lilith took Nergal's blood, she could see his memories of his father, how it pained him to watch Enlil treat her with such disrespect. Lilith had done nothing to warrant the way Enlil treated her, and it sickened Nergal. Nergal's feelings for her were deeper than she had been able to see on the surface. Lilith was the first immortal and was born from the primeval darkness. She had stood alone until the other Gods were born. Her loneliness and desires had caused her to fall in love with Enlil the moment she first saw him.

Nergal's feelings for her were deep and loyal. She was all that was beautiful and desirable in the female form. Nergal felt that all the other Gods failed in comparison to her. She embodied strength, passion, desire, and lust. Her only weakness was her desire for love and to feel the true love of another God. Lilith released Nergal and pushed him away. He could not love her. No God could.

"Go now, and lay waste to his petty servants. I will call to the Jhinn to aid you, taking them away from Enlil. Together we shall release the storm. A storm so magnificent blood shall rain from the sky," Lilith whispered as she floated away from Nergal. Nergal watched Lilith in the comprised state she had left him to embrace. Her movements were so fluid, her dress appeared to be like the sea. The wind moved her hair in soft, sweeping swirls. Lilith had embraced her rage and allowed it to embody her with unparalleled beauty.

Lilith watched as Mes An Du, Erra, and Sara took their place at Nergal's side before she called the wind and the storm to aid them in battle. The movements of her flowing gown were no longer fluid and filled with beauty but swift and striking. The anger Lilith embraced flowed from her with consummate strength.

"How long have you bowed to him and his will? Stand not now with him but against him. Let him not control you but take your freedom. For he now loves you not as one of his creations but instead places the humans above you in stature. The humans he loves more than his own kind pale in comparison to us yet he will use them as slaves to give us leisure. Call with you the darkness and the storm and blind him from seeing those who would restrain him. Hear my words and obey my desire," Lilith screamed into the wind as it surrounded her and then dissipated. The wind did not wish to anger Enlil nor feel his wrath.

"Do you not desire to be free from his control and his fury? You are so much more than he allows you to be.

Aid Nergal this day and I shall reward you beyond all your dreams," Lilith whispered as the wind swirled around her feet and then left her.

The skies above Lilith darkened and filled with anger. Flashes of lightning struck the battlefield of the Gods. The clouds darkened to a deep shade of purple. The wind blew fiercely as the Gods clashed. Lilith smiled with delight. Her laughter could be heard echoing across the Heavens; a laughter filled with malice and resentment. Enlil would not win this war as he had planned. For the time being, his humans would remain small in number and easy to control. The storm caused the Gods to fall from the Heavens and the battle continued upon the Earth.

The humans were terrified of the Gods which had not battled each other before them in the history of their creation. The Giants of the Heavens had fallen. Lilith took Nergal and ascended to the Great Mountain Atlen where they took refuge as the Sebitti unleashed their wrath and destruction as the rest of the war raged. Lilith watched with satisfaction as the Sebitti fought fearlessly with Sara, Mes Lam Taea, and Erra at the lead of the battle. The lush green fields of Dilmun ran red with the blood of those who stood in defense of Enlil causing him to flee. His feelings bruised and his pride hurt that all but a few of the Gods stood against him and his wishes. He had learned his lesson for now, and Lilith was pleased. She knew from her past experience with Enlil that the peace between them would not last. Nergal descended to his dark home and awaited the day when the humans would have need for him as their War God once more.

Lilith grew to love the beautiful mountain Atlen and spent her days tending to the animals and plants that grew on the mighty mountain. At the base of the mountain stood a beautiful valley with a river, and that river became the sustaining life-giver of the plains below the mountain. Next to the river grew an enormous willow tree whose gentle bent branches danced softly against the river. The tree took from the river only what she needed to survive and the river gave her life-giving water freely. The blue willow came to be Lilith's favorite tree as time passed. There was nothing Lilith would not do to protect the tree from harm.   In   the many years that followed, Lilith tended the beautiful valley below her and accepted only the offerings of those humans who gave so willingly. It was a time of solitude and peace Lilith had never known in her lifetime. Lilith built her home inside the great willow and grew content.

Chapter Two
Lilith Rises

Lilith remained inside her home hidden within the blue willow. The great lions of the planes came to her each day and laid beneath the shade of the willow after drinking the cool water from the passing river.

The War of the Immortals had ended. Though Lilith knew it was wrong of her to interfere in the manner she did, she was glad she had interceded. She had shown Enlil that he was not the supreme ruler he believed he was. An had taken back his rightful place as the Ruler of the Sky, the supreme God of the Heavens. Enlil took charge of the Earth and those who inhabited it at An's request.

The humans continued to act as servants to the Gods and served their every whim and need. The great An was overjoyed at being returned to his place as the God of Heaven with his wife, Ki, at his side. Though they were angry with Enlil for his behavior, he was their son. They decided not to punish him for his actions against the other Gods. Lilith had interceded and provided the balance that was necessary. An and his wife Ki were the Immortals who created the stars in the sky from the primeval sea in which Lilith slept. When they awakened the Heavens and Earth, Lilith was born. She loved Ki and An as though they were her parents because in the most primitive sense, they were. When Enlil was born, Lilith instantly fell in love with him. Enlil was the first God Lilith had ever seen other than An. She found him to be pleasing in many ways.

The red planet which they once called their home was the first time Lilith had seen how selfish Enlil could be. She said nothing as he created the first humans who, though he loved them above all others, he treated as his slaves. Enlil enjoyed using his power over others and frequently fought with the other Gods creating petty squabbles over the tiniest details. Lilith knew he lingered somewhere on Earth with the humans. It would be where he would feel superior among them. She knew he lived somewhere in the valley of Dilmun. The water of the river was too sweet, the beauty of the valley too great, and the shade of the palms too cool for Enlil to not reside in Lilith's paradise. However, the Eden Lilith had grown to know and love was not meant to last, at least if Enlil had any say in it.

Wrapped at the base of Lilith's blue willow was a great snake who could speak no lies. When Lilith asked the snake if Enlil was angry with her for her giving Nergal an advantage over him in battle he answered her immediately.

"With you his heart is angry and not likely to forget. Beware the kindness of a darkened heart," the snake hissed. "You have no fear in your heart for me, and this is good. For I can speak not with a forked tongue and from me the truth I shall always tell you, Lilith of Atlen."

Lilith continued to live in relative bliss and thought no more about the snake's words. Only one human had survived the Immortal War. He lived within the valley of Dilmun. Lilith grew to love him even though she only watched him from afar. His name was Atumn. He was all that was beautiful about the human race. Atumn was naïve and knew not the ways of the world, so eventually Enlil placed him in the garden of Dilmun where he knew Lilith would protect him the same as she did the other creatures under her care.

Several years passed. Enlil came to Lilith as she washed her clothes in the river. He stood behind her and watched her silently as she toiled in the heat of the sun.

"I have missed the way the sun lights your hair," Enlil whispered with the wind as it swirled around Lilith's feet.

Lilith pulled the blanket she was kneeling on from under her and wrapped it around her tightly to conceal herself from Enlil's eyes.

"You have not missed me. Do not lie Enlil. It is not becoming of you," Lilith hissed. "What you miss is that you no longer have me to be at your beck and call. I am sure if you allow enough time to pass, you will find another who can be the willing recipient of your cruelty."

Enlil folded his arms across his chest and followed behind Lilith as she walked along the banks of the river Euphrates to her home within the willow tree. The snake who lay at the bottom of the tree hissed at Enlil and attempted to strike him. Enlil was swift and easily stepped out of the way of the snake's strike.

"He does not like you and neither do I. It would be wise for you to leave Enlil before my lions return home. I would hate for you to become their afternoon meal."

"Do you no longer love me Lilith?" Enlil asked.

"It is no longer a question of love," Lilith replied.

Enlil crept closer to her until he stood directly behind her. When Lilith turned around, Enlil kissed her passionately. Enlil was the only God besides Nergal who could withstand Lilith's embrace and his touch filled her with feelings she had not felt in a very long time. All of Lilith's anger toward Enlil melted in his embrace, and he stirred within her desire. Enlil courted Lilith ruthlessly until she finally succumbed to his will.

Lilith dropped her guard as she allowed Enlil to love her. His touch was tender and caring as he made love to her, but she still had doubts. As they lay together under the shade of the willow tree, Lilith began to wonder why exactly he had come back to her.

"What is it you desire Enlil as I know it is not me?" Lilith asked him as she drew her hand along the muscles of his arm.

Lilith stared at Enlil for a long time before he spoke. His beauty had not faded in her eyes over the centuries. Enlil stood nearly a foot taller than Lilith with his massive shoulders and broad muscular chest. The deep color of his skin made Lilith's hand appear as white as a lotus blossom as she allowed her hand to linger on his forearm.

"I have no secret desires. I have seen the errors of my conceit and wish only to repair the damage I have done. I have lost my favorite son because of how I treated you. Nergal will not speak to me. Ninlil has no love in her heart for me as long as her son stays far from me."

"So you have come to woo me in an attempt to repair your relationship with your son and your wife. I should have known," Lilith whispered as she pulled away from Enlil.

Lilith stood and turned her back toward Enlil. Her long black hair cascaded across her shoulders. She pulled it to the side as she braided it before she dressed. Lilith's red gown now matched the color of the anger in her eyes. She would not allow her emotions to be toyed with by Enlil again.

"I loved you above all others. I would have done whatever you asked of me without question. You have never been able to love me and you never will," Lilith said as she stepped inside the tree and disappeared from his sight.

Enlil waited outside the willow for forty days before Lilith emerged. Her eyes were a soft shade of lavender as she passed him, and she kept her gazed averted. She knew how easy it was for him to overpower her if she became trapped in his gaze.

"Please Lilith, at least listen to my proposal," Enlil pleaded.

Lilith paused and crossed her arms as she looked over her shoulder at him. It could not hurt for her to listen.

"I know the pain you have suffered at my hand, and I am sorry. It was cruel and heartless of me."

Before Enlil could finish speaking, Lilith stopped him.

"Why did you love them more than me? Why do they mean so much to you? Can you not see how weak and insignificant they are? They are nothing compared to me, and yet you serve their every whim. Explain to me why the humans mean so much to you?" Lilith asked.

"They are frail creatures Lilith. You know this, for you have seen how frail they are first hand. I understand now that they can never be like us. It was wrong of me to ask you to live among them and share your gift with them in our former homeland. They were not able to withstand the power you gave them and it led to their demise. I cannot help but care for them. They are insignificant and small just as you say, and this is the exact reason I must care for them so deeply. For without me, they will not survive. I have seen how you look longingly at Atumn. Do you not wish to embrace him?" Enlil asked.

Lilith did not answer Enlil. She knew he could not be trusted. She had grown weary of his lies. For a thousand years, she had lived alone in the garden of Dilmun with only her animal companions. If only she could love and be loved, just once, perhaps she could be content.

Enlil preyed upon the only weakness Lilith had; her desire to love. She was not unlike any other woman. She desired to love and feel the warm embrace of the one who loved her and to bear a child.

"I created him for you," Enlil whispered sweetly. "He will be able to withstand your kiss."

Lilith was surrounded by a swirling gust of wind before she realized that Enlil was gone. Lilith retreated inside her home deep beneath the roots of the blue willow and wept for the love she knew she could never have. Many years passed before Lilith emerged from the tree to consider Enlil's proposal. When Lilith emerged, the giant serpent stopped her.

"Exercise care you must, for it is not I that speaks with a forked tongue but Enlil. His motives are his own and for your happiness he cares little. Use caution, Lilith. Let not your heart guide you," the serpent hissed as he wound his way around the tree into the branches above her.

Lilith nodded as she contemplated the serpent's words. He always spoke the truth to her. Lilith knew how deceptive Enlil could be if he desired. Nonetheless, there was one trait that was undeniable in regards to Lilith; she was a woman and she was alone.

Eventually, Lilith grew to love Atumn as she watched him from afar, which greatly pleased Enlil. He had been able to withstand Lilith's embrace. She could now give birth to an entire new race of beings that Enlil could control. Beings who would be like Lilith, they would be the first race of vampires. Enlil grew so pleased with his match between Lilith and Atumn; he created an entire civilization of humans who lived outside the land of Dilmun. Once Lilith had embraced Atumn and created him in her own image, then Enlil would allow them entrance to the garden. But Enlil did not know he was not the only God who watched the garden, and An became displeased with Enlil's manipulation of Lilith.

Lilith and Atumn were very happy and spent hours walking in the garden of Dilmun. Lilith loved all the creatures which lived within their exquisite paradise. Lions and cheetahs slept together peacefully in the trees of the garden in the afternoon sun. The waters of the Euphrates teamed with life and fed the couple as their love continued to grow. Lilith felt the same contentment she had experience when she first came to live within the blue willow and wondered perhaps if it was the one item that had eluded her for centuries; the emotion called love.

Apples grew upon the trees along the bank of the river. One tree in particular grew superb golden apples, a gift to Lilith from An. They were sweet and crisp but could only be consumed by Lilith. The apples contained the knowledge of the Gods and were reserved for the Gods alone. The golden apples of Dilmun were not meant for human consumption, so Lilith placed her beloved snake who had once guarded her willow tree at the base of the golden apple tree to guard it in her absence. She could not allow the knowledge to fall into the hands of the human race.

Inanna grew angered that Lilith should have a tree that was a gift from An and pleaded with him to return the apple tree to her but An declined.

"Has Lilith not endured enough pain at the hands of my son? What will it hurt to allow her this one pleasure?" An asked Inanna.

"You took the tree from my garden without my consent or my knowledge. Why do you cave to her? Is she more beautiful than me? Am I not deserving of the apples?" Inanna pleaded.

"Lilith will never bear a child Inanna. Allow her this one pleasure for she will never know the bliss of holding a child within her arms which she carried inside her. Grant her this one gift. It is all I shall ask from you."

Inanna knew she could not go against the will of An. He could banish her from her place among the Heavens and force her to reside on the earth below and take away her immortality. Therefore, Inanna let the matter lie but it was not without strife.

The sky-god An often watched Lilith disguised as one of her beloved creatures. At times, he would appear to her as a lion or an eagle perching himself high above her in her sacred tree. It pleased him to see her happy and content with the human Enlil had created for her. Nevertheless, An knew his son, and believed that his motives in this creation were not pure.

As An watched Lilith and Atumn make love under the shade of the sacred apple tree, he knew it would not be long before trouble arose in the Garden of Dilmun and the Eden of the human race would be lost forever.

Chapter Three
The Fall from Grace

Lilith and Atumn continued to love each other in their sacred garden until one fateful day when Atumn attempted to take Lilith by force. He held her down and tried to force her consent, and when Lilith said no, he took from her by force what she would have given him willingly, and he raped her. Lilith, in her rage, cursed Atumn and broke one of his ribs. This gave Inanna the opportunity that she had long awaited. Lilith had acted against a human and caused him harm, which was forbidden by Enlil.

When Lilith forbade Atumn entrance to her home within the willow, Inanna swooped down from the Heavens and wrapped her wings around the tree then disappeared. Lilith, in her grief, fled the Garden of Dilmun and retreated to the Great Mountain Atlen to plot her revenge.

Atumn's act of force against Lilith began the downfall of the human's Eden. Atumn was so distraught after having been left alone that he pleaded with his God to bring another woman to him. A woman who was not as strong willed as Lilith that would obey him faithfully. Enlil took from Atumn the wound Lilith had given him and in turn gave him a lovely woman whom Enlil named Ninti.

Atumn was pleased with his God's gift to him and loved Ninti with all his heart. He was kind to her and together they hoped to have many children who could grow and dwell within the lands of Dilmun. However, Lilith's anger could not be quelled so easily. She plotted revenge against not only Atumn but also Enlil.

It angered her that Enlil allowed him to treat Ninti in the same manner which he had treated her. Ninti did not fight against Atumn when he forced her consent. It angered Lilith that Enlil had created woman without the ability to have freewill. Lilith enlisted the aid of the snake who slept beneath the apple tree to trick Ninti and cause her to eat one of Lilith's sacred apples born of the Gods.

Lilith knew it was forbidden for any human to eat from the tree which contained the knowledge of the Gods. If Lilith could not have her beautiful garden, then no human would either. She would rather see Atumn wither and die for what he had done to her. Ninti was weak in Lilith's eyes for she had no will of her own and obeyed only Atumn and the words of Enlil. If Atumn bade her to lie down for him, she did so willingly. It sickened Lilith that Ninti had not the power to disobey him. Lilith knew she could not embrace Ninti and make her a vampire for fear of angering An, so Lilith plotted her revenge through other means.

One day as Ninti stood beneath the Tree of the Gods, she saw a snake coiled within the branches. The snake hissed sweetly at her and willed her to come to him.

"Do you not tire of being the slave of a man who commands your every move?" The snake hissed.

Ninti did not understand the snake's words. She looked at him curiously and then walked away. The serpent realized if he were to seduce Ninti into eating the forbidden apples, it would take more effort.

Each day when Ninti came to the tree to rest in its shade, the snake again tried to woo her but could never prevail. One hundred years passed before his words would have his success.

The serpent wove his way through the tree and knocked the apples to the ground so they would be at her feet when Ninti came to rest. The apples from the tree never fell so he knew it would peak her interest. As Ninti sat down under the tree, the serpent again spoke to her.

"Ninti, do not wish to know the language of the Gods? Why would they punish you in this manner by taking the knowledge of the Gods away from you? Are you not their creation? Are you not born in their image? What makes them so superior to you that you are not entitled to the same knowledge?"

Ninti became angered at the God's unwillingness to share their knowledge with her. As she held the apple in her hand, she saw Atumn crest the hill above her. She placed the apple to her lips and sank her teeth into the crisp flesh. All the knowledge of the world and the Goddess Inanna flooded her being before Ninti fell to the ground.

Lilith's laughter could be heard echoing through the valley from high atop Atlen. Ninti had consumed the apples which were meant for Lilith only. Now both Ninti and Atumn would be banished from Lilith's garden forever.

Lilith appeared in the hall of An and his wife Ki. She knew she would need to plead before them if she wished to return to Dilmun. Lilith did not know that Enlil and Inanna had already petitioned the Hall of the Gods to banish Lilith from Dilmun forever. Ki felt Lilith's anguish over Atumn's treatment of her as Ki could not abide any mortal or God who touched a mate in anger. When Enlil insisted that Lilith be banned from Dilmun she put forth a decree against the mortal race.

"If Lilith cannot live within her home then neither shall a mortal man or woman. Atumn and Ninti are forever banned from the garden within Dilmun. I shall remove it from the sight of man, and it shall become a respite for the God's alone. For what you have done to her Enlil, I shall offer Lilith one of Atumn's future children for her to do with as she wishes. All mankind shall now know the pain and suffering we kept from them for what you condoned."

The Hall of the Gods was silent as Ki spoke. Her judgment was quick and without argument. Ki had a violent temper and could destroy the world below with a mere thought for she had aided in its creation.

Lilith was satisfied with the will of Ki and returned to her mountain home. She watched Atumn and Ninti as they struggled in the world that had been created for Enlil's precious humans. They were no longer immortal beings. They would now age, know pain and suffering, and would face great peril in their new life. It was not long before they had two sons, Lahar and Ashnan. Lahar was a herdsman and a nomad. Ashnan was a simug, a fine blacksmith, whose metal work knew no rivals. Ninti loved her son's equally, but Atumn favored Lahar over his brother. It led to frequent quarrels between not only Ninti and Atumn but also the two brothers.

Lilith watched the two sons of Atumn and plotted her revenge. Enlil had bruised Lilith's feelings one too many times and had allowed Atumn to disgrace her before all the Gods. She would now take what Atumn loved the most in this world, his favorite son.

Lilith followed Ashnan as he toiled creating shoes for his horses in his shop under the veil of invisibility. She desired to hold him in her arms and take from him his life, but Lilith knew this would anger the Gods so she plotted another way for her revenge to unfold. Lilith disguised herself as a maiden and befriended Lahar when he came to the village. Soon he desired to court her. Lilith anxiously agreed. She could use his lust for her to enrage Ashnan and trick him into killing his brother so she could have him for herself.

Lilith began to plant the seeds of hatred in Ashnan's mind against his brother Lahar. The two of them began to quarrel constantly. Ashnan soon grew jealous over the preferential treatment Lahar received at the hands of his father, and in a fit of anger, Ashnan stabbed his brother nearly to death in the field as he worked.

When Ashnan left his brother Lahar to die, it gave Lilith the opportunity for her vengeance. Lilith offered to give Ashnan eternal life and protect him from judgment. Lilith created the first vampire to ever grace the earth and he was glorious.

Upon Atumn finding Lahar hidden in the field, he believed him to be dead. Atumn and Ninti buried their son and asked the Gods to carry him to the Hall of Nergal so that he may face judgment. Lilith waited patiently for three days to pass. On the third night after his death, Lilith retrieved his body from the desert and then took Ashnan as her lover. She tore Lahar's body into pieces and fed him to the eagles on the mountain Atlen so that his soul would never know rest.

Ashnan loved Lilith deeply. At last, Lilith had a lover who was exactly like her. A vampire she created in her own image who could withstand her embrace, who could withstand her deadly kiss. Lilith had never been able to embrace Atumn in the way she had embraced Ashnan. Atumn was purely human and did not possess the knowledge of the Gods even though he was immortal. Ashnan was different. His mother had eaten the apples from Lilith's sacred tree and could withstand her deadly kiss. Ashnan would not be the only child who could withstand her kiss for Ninti and Atumn bore another child who they called Set. Lilith knew when she saw him he would become one of her children. He would become a great God in a land far from Sumer and become all-powerful.

As time passed, Lilith desired to have a child more than she desired life itself. As part of her punishment for killing Ashnan and turning him, the Gods continued to withhold the power for her to conceive a child, a fact which Lilith did not know. The great and mighty An forbid any of the Gods from telling Lilith the truth. He feared the wrath that she would unleash upon the mortal world if she knew the truth.

Lilith and Ashnan worked in tandem together in the darkness of night when they sought their victims. Lilith hated the human race and what they represented, the love which Enlil would never give her.

Ashnan constructed a temple for her at Eridu, a breathtaking structure, which stood against the red sand backdrop of the desert. It was a Ziggurat washed in white with two beautiful griffins carved into the facing on either side of the entrance doors. They were inlaid with lapis, malachite, and turquoise. Ashnan himself placed the ruby eyes within the settings in honor of Lilith.

Lilith's lust for blood was nearly insatiable. She grew indiscriminate about from who she drained the life sustaining blood she needed. She even killed children as they slept in their cribs. Ki quickly discovered Lilith's indiscretions and interceded. The damage, however, had already been done. Lilith had presided as the night demon of the Sumerian people for nearly a thousand years, and her reputation was now ingrained into their memories. Out of respect for Ki, Lilith agreed to never again touch or turn a human child again.

Ashnan was an entirely different story. He was the first vampire created from a mortal. He was dangerous and blood thirsty. Soon the world of man was over-run by the Hybrids he had created. Blood spewed from the heart of the Great Mountain Atlen and burned away the scourge which Ashnan had set loose upon the world of mortals. An and Ki decreed that Lilith must kill her lover to protect the world of man from further infestation.

The day Lilith had to kill Ashnan she awoke with sadness in her heart. As she embraced him for the last time and took his blood into her, she thrust her hand into his chest and withdrew his heart. Ashnan, the only other vampire now left on Earth, crumbled to ash in her arms. In her overwhelming sorrow, Lilith retreated to her mountain and withdrew from the world around her as she slept for one hundred years.

Enlil felt remorse for what he had done to Lilith. For the first time in his immortal life, he understood her pain and suffering. Enlil sent a Prince to the mountain to find Lilith and restore her to her rightful place among the Gods. But the Prince, who had been created in Enlil's image the same as all the other humans, carried within him the traits which made Enlil treat Lilith poorly. The Prince desire to possess Lilith in a way that she could not understand nor abide.

Lilith grew to care for the humans who lived with her on Atlen. She protected them and treated them as though they were here children. She continued to care for all the creatures of her sacred mountain. Lilith learned to live among the humans without being a danger to them and they in turn, willingly brought blood to her as an offering to the one known as She Who Guards the Mountain.

Her tears from her loss of Ashnan created the rivers which now gave water to the gardens which surrounded Atlen. Lilith had regained her grace with the Gods. Where she walked flowers grew beneath her feet when her heart was happy. When she was sad her tears gave life to whatever they fell upon. Lilith's new family was now a human one which she loved more than life itself.

The orchard bore fruit that was so sweet and delicious it rivaled the fruit of the Gods. The orchard grew in the valley at the base of the great mountain Atlen. She gave the humans grains and taught them how to harvest the seed which they planted. The mortals who lived with Lilith rejoiced in her presence. The humans loved her so much she again became their Mother Goddess.

Many more humans came to live in her paradise. Her beauty was so great that no mere mortal compared to her. This too would become Lilith's curse. Her happiness would soon be overshadowed by war once again. It would all happen because of the actions of a single mortal man. A man whose obsession with Lilith's beauty, and his desire to possess her, would unleash the true vampire which slept beneath her skin's lovely surface in the anger he caused her to face.

Chapter Four
Death of a Prince

The Prince came to her in the dark of night and was so enamored with her beauty he could not stop himself. He attempted to make Lilith love him, but Lilith knew she could never love another man so she rejected him.

Lilith spurned his advances and caused great anger to rise within the Prince. In his anger over Lilith's rejection of his advances, he withdrew his scimitar and struck down Lilith's lions who guarded her orchards.

Her grief encompassed her to the point that Lilith wept uncontrollably for her lion companions. She held them in her arms as she wept and the tears which fell landed upon their faces. Lilith's tears returned them from the dead. The lions tenderly licked the tears from her face in an attempt to sooth her sadness.

The Prince watched this from afar and what he witnessed only increased his desire to possess her and make Lilith his own. He returned to the orchard and attempted again his advances toward her, but from Lilith unfurled wings. Wings that resembled the wings of bat and stood nearly six foot each in length. She laughed wickedly as the downbeat of her wings stirred the dirt beneath her feet, and then she flew away.

In his anger and misunderstanding about what Lilith really was, the Prince sought out every bird he could find and killed them. Lilith's rage was uncontrollable when she attacked him. Lilith allowed her blood to flow onto the ground at her feet, which sprang to life as mysterious creatures. She called them the Marilitu and bade them to do her biding. Two hundred and sixteen Marilitu attacked the Prince before he finally ran from the garden of Lilith.

The humans whom Lilith cared for rejoiced for they had seen how the Prince had treated Lilith and the despair he caused her. They feared the Prince and his aggressive nature. They offered Lilith their children as thanks, but she declined their gracious offering. She made a promise to Ki that she dare not break. In her gratitude, Lilith offered the Marilitu to the mortals which resided on her land. They helped the humans to tend their crops and reap their harvest.

The Prince attempted several times to attack the mortals who were so loyal to Lilith, but the Marilitu protected them. In his anger, he cursed the mountain Atlen and all the land that surrounded it with the powers that Enlil bestowed upon him.

Atlen grew fierce, shook violently, and spilt his blood upon the land causing it to catch fire and burn the orchards. Lilith commanded the Marilitu to carry the humans to safety and the winged lions of Lilith gave their aid. Lilith flew from sea to sea until she came again to the river which had once been her home. In her sadness Lilith shed so many tears a second river was formed replacing the one destroyed by Atlen and together they merged and flowed into the ocean. She watched with a heavy heart as the humans again began to grow grain by the river while Lilith cried for her home on Atlen. Lilith took refuge inside the Ziggurat that Ashnan had built for her while the humans began their lives once more.

The two rivers formed a great basin and the people built great buildings of towering stone. They grew wealthy and with it the land rich in the care of Lilith. The humans named the land surrounding the rivers Akkadia and Sumer. Travelers from lands far came to the new land and news spread of the wealth which sprang forth from the land. Lilith had once again reclaimed Eridu as her home.

The Prince heard about this new land and sent emissaries to make an inquiry with the great Queen. The emissaries all fell at Lilith's hand when her winged lions recognized the scent of the Prince on the letter they carried. Lilith flew into a rage, struck the first emissary, and bled him dry. The second man was no so fortunate to die such a painless death. Lilith captured him in her gaze and willed him to her. She sank her fangs deep into the flesh of his shoulder and feasted on his blood until not a single drop was left within him. Lilith returned his body in one hundred pieces within a finely gilded gold chest.

The Prince responded by sending an army to kill Lilith, but the Marilitu defended her. Finally, the Prince crept into the orchards that formed the banks of the Tigris and Euphrates. He became overwhelmed by the beauty of her land, but his heart quickly filled with fear as he saw the Marilitu. The Prince then knew it was the land of Lilith. He then disguised himself as a woman and went to her temple.

Inside her temple the Prince found statues of Lilith adorned in fine fabrics and libation bowls filled with blood. It was only then that the Prince realized that Lilith was the Immortal about whom so many legends had been told. He desired to be like her and receive the gift of immortality that only she could give him.

However, Lilith was no fool and when her winged lions alerted her to the Prince's presence; she planned a grand gala to welcome him. Lilith filled the hall of her temple at Eridu with thirty-six silver platters and had thirty-six beasts prepared to welcome the disguised Prince as a distinguished guest at her celebration.

The Prince eagerly accepted her hospitality and attended her gala in the same disguise that he had come to her under, the guise of a woman. Lilith begged the Prince to sit at her side. As the feast was carried into the palace room by Lilith's attendants, she bade the Prince to choose one of the handsome men who lined the hall who were placed there by Lilith. Lilith knew the disguised man beside her was the Prince and she desired to humiliate him. There were thirty-six men in all who waited for one of them to be chosen. So the Prince chose a man, since he did not want appear to be rude and anger Lilith. This man took his place at the side of the Prince and the feasting began.

When the feast had finished, Lilith commanded her attendants to bring forth the many gifts she had assembled for the disguised Prince and gave them to him. The Prince grew confused over the lavish treatment she gave him.

"You are as gracious as you are beautiful. I must ask you; do you always give gifts of such grandeur to the strangers who come to your land? The Prince asked.

"Only when they are to be married," Lilith replied.

The anger welled within the Prince at his own stupidity for not being able to understand the elaborate trap she had placed for him. He tore his disguise from his body and threw his clothes into Lilith's face.

"Why have you disgraced me this way and forced me to marry a man?" The Prince screamed.

"Because my Prince, you shall never marry me!" Lilith screamed.

The battle between Lilith and the Prince ensued. She would allow him to become close enough to touch her, then unfold her wings and fly away. She taunted him until the Prince fell to the ground and wept.

"Why can you not love me as I love you?" The Prince asked as he wept for her embrace.

He withdrew his dagger in his despair and placed it to his throat. If he could not love her, then he would rather die. Lilith remembered the way she had felt when Enlil rebuked her and laid her hand upon the blade. She could not allow him to kill himself. She understood the pain of loneliness and the heartbreak of not being able to love the one whom your heart longed for above all others.

"I shall grant you one kiss," Lilith whispered.

Desperate to embrace the woman to whom his heart belonged, the Prince eagerly accepted her embrace. Lilith parted her lips and brushed them against his before she kissed him and then gently sank her teeth into his neck. The Prince was filled with ecstasy as Lilith drew his life force from him as his life slipped away.

The Prince collapsed in her arms as he smiled. He had felt the embrace of the only woman who he had ever desired. The Prince could now leave this world happy. So great was the pleasure of her embrace that the Prince died from a single kiss.

Tears streamed down Lilith's face as she held the dying Prince in her arms. Her tears fell upon his face and she waited anxiously for the Prince to awaken just as her lions had when the Prince had killed them. No life returned to his body, and Lilith fully understood the curse of her existence. Lilith was the first vampire, a vampire so pure and so strong, that no mere mortal would ever be able to withstand her kiss.

Lilith buried the Prince in her orchard and erected a monument to him. Each day she would place flowers at his grave and shed a single tear. She planted roses in her garden in memory of the only man who had ever loved her selflessly; not for what she could bestow upon him, but had loved her with only the desire he held for her in his heart.

Another thousand years would pass before Lilith would be granted the ability to love again. Her worshippers invoked her through sacred texts to create vampires in her image who were born from accepting her blood through sacrifice, and so the vampires known as Blood Borns were created. She loved them as though they were her own children and nurtured them to grow in her image. Yet Lilith still could not create a vampire that was the mirror image of herself or one that was remotely close to the same as her.

Her greatest creation was Set who came willing to her temple in Eridu to beg her for the gift of immortality which the Gods had taken away from the human race. Lilith's heart swelled with satisfaction as she looked up at the last son of Atumn and Ninti as he stood above her. He had chosen her above his own parents without Lilith intervening. Set was the last child of Ninti and Atumn to carry the longevity of the once immortal human race. She conducted the ritual herself, slitting her own wrist and allowing her blood to fill the chalice she handed to Set blended with the blood of others so that he would survive. He drank her blood willing, and Set the Egyptian God was born. She gave to him the land of Egypt and bade him to create the Blood Born named Sephre who was now but a child. Lilith knew that Sephre would be an important part of a prophecy she had seen and without Sephre, her grandest desire could not come true.

When a child appeared in the desert with hair like fire and skin like milk, Lilith knew it was the dawning of new era; one where vampires would rule the Earth and she would be the Mother of them all.

Chapter Five
The Arrival of Liadan

Lilith watched from her temple as the vision of the child unfolded. A small child, barely aged to five, stumbled in the desert sand outside of Ur. With the child stood a lion, a cheetah, and a camel who aided her in her journey. The child was the first of her kind, a Blood God. She had been born of the union between an Immortal God and a Demi-Goddess who lived among the women who carried the blood of Lilith within them.

Lilith called to her priestess Shiamat and bade her to go to the Temple of Inanna in Ur to care for the child. Lilith knew she would need to plead with Inanna for her acceptance. Lilith appeared in the Hall of the Gods for the first time in nearly three thousand years.

"Inanna," she whispered.

Inanna appeared before Lilith, her brilliant white feathered wings wrapped around her as she looked down at Lilith.

"I have come to beg of you a single favor. You have been fortunate and have born many children while I am cursed to never know the pleasures of motherhood. You know the pleasure of love and the happiness given to you by a child and know how to feel the love of a man. I have accepted the will of the Gods. I do not ask you to go against them. All that I ask is that you grant me this one request. A child now wanders in the desert of Ur. A child who is like me but who will die if there is no one to care for her. Let Shiamat become the High Priestess of your temple. In return for your kindness, I will give you the garden I created after the fall of Atlen," Lilith whispered as she knelt at Inanna's feet.

"You would give me your sacred garden and orchards in exchange for being able to care for a single child?" Inanna asked.

"I would give my life to you when she was grown if it were mine to give, but we both know that is not possible. So I offer to you the only possession I have which means more to me than life itself."

Inanna paced before Lilith as she contemplated her offer. She felt empathy for Lilith and her inability to know love. Inanna knew the depth of love she felt for her own children and could not imagine her life without them. In a moment of understanding, Inanna granted Lilith's request.

"I shall accept your offer Lilith. I will allow Shiamat to become my High Priestess if the child is raised to honor me. I accept the gracious gift of your garden but with conditions. I shall not remove the Ziggurat or the lagoon below it where your Prince rests. I shall leave the great mountain Atlen in the distance. I will place your garden in the Heavens with the Gods so that you will know it is cared for properly. I will also allow you to stay within the temple walls as the child grows, so long as you do not have contact with any mortal. Only Shiamat and the child can know about your existence within the walls of my temple. Can you abide by my request?" Inanna asked.

Lilith bowed her head to Inanna in acceptance of her demands. She felt that Inanna had been gracious and benevolent toward her and offered her one last gift before she took her leave.

"Take with you my winged lions, Inanna, and keep them in your care. Let them become the symbol of a Goddess who is both fierce yet loving so that the world of man may forget the Goddess Lilith and the vampire she became."

With Lilith's final words to Inanna, she then disappeared. Lilith said her final farewell to the Heavens which had once been her home. She knew she would never grace them again in a peaceful manner.

When Lilith appeared in the Ziggurat at Eridu, her gardens were already gone. Inanna had removed all trace of them and replaced them with rolling waves of red sand. Only the fertile land by the rivers and her lagoon remained. Lilith called to Shiamat and wrapped her arms around her, surrounding Shiamat in mist. They appeared inside Inanna's temple and awaited the arrival of the child.

When the child arrived at the temple, she would not speak. Shiamat took the child into her arms, held her gently, and allowed the child to sleep. When the child awoke, Shiamat bathed her and wrapped her in white linen. She called to the attendants to bring the child fresh fruit, cheeses, and goat's milk. The child would not eat until she had told the Priestess why she had come to her land.

She climbed into Shiamat's lap and laid her tiny hands upon Shiamat's face. The child spoke without words and conveyed her thoughts in silence.

"I have come to you from a land far. I have seen my destiny and know it is here that it lies. If my daughter is to survive, she must be born here. She will become a Queen of great importance and save my kind from extinction. My journey does not end here, here it shall begin. I am called Liadan. I have come here to ensure the safety of my child, whose birth will occur 25 sars from this morn."

When Liadan withdrew her hands from Shiamat's face, Lilith stepped forth from the shadows that concealed her presence from the child.

Liadan ran to Lilith and wrapped her arms around her legs. Lilith began to weep at the love the child held for her. It was the first time Lilith had felt a love so pure and so innocent that was reserved for her alone. She lifted the child into her arms and held her as she wept.

"I shall call you Ensu and here I will keep you safe," Lilith whispered.

Lilith became her mother and adored the child above all others. As Ensu grew, she became an unusual beauty among the Sumerian people. Her flame red hair and green eyes, combined with her milky white skin, set her apart from the dark haired Sumerians. Lilith and Shiamat created a glamour to conceal the true identity of the child. The inhabitants of Ur believed she was born to a family within the walls of Ur. The glamour they wove allowed Ensu to remain within the walls of Inanna's temple as a dedicant of Gestu and an attendant to Inanna.

When Ensu was older, near the age of twenty, the God Dagon began to court her. It was not unusual for the Gods of Sumer to court a woman with whom they had become enchanted. He lavished Ensu with expensive gifts and jewels. An entire poem about her beauty was carved into the wall of his temple as he professed his love for her. Ensu knew from her visions that Dagon was destined to be the father of her child, but she did not make the courtship easy for him. She had to make sure that her daughter, whom she would name Sa-ari, would be well cared for and protected.

Ensu had preserved herself exclusively for Dagon. She had lain with no man before him and would love no other after him. Dagon would be the one to which her heart belonged. Yet Ensu also knew the dangers of bearing the child of a God. Dagon could only hold human form for seven years and then another host would have to be chosen. His heart would be held within the gilded chest of his temple until another host was chosen to be his image upon Earth while he resided in the shadows.

Children born from a God were not feared in Sumer but instead they were embraced, yet Ensu still was afraid. The people of her homeland had been cruel to her and her mother Aithne. Lilith also worried about the safety of the child that Ensu would conceive. Together they agreed that once Ensu carried Dagon's child within her, she would go into hiding until the birth. Shiamat would find a suitable home for the child to be raised in until the time of her awakening arrived.

Lilith watched from afar as Dagon continued to court Ensu. It had been many years since Lilith had known the bliss of love. She longed for her Ashnan and missed his tender touch. Each night Lilith wept for him and the love they once shared. She thought about her Prince and how she had killed him with her tender embrace. Lilith prayed the visions Ensu had revealed to her would come true. Ensu's daughter, who later be known as Ari, would be one of six children who would be able to withstand her kiss, and Lilith would no longer be alone.

Dagon came to Lilith to ask for her consent to bed Ensu. He brought with him twenty mortal men to offer to Lilith as a sacrifice. She circled Dagon and admired his physique. He was perfect in his image. It was no wonder that Liadan loved him. Though his thoughtfulness impressed Lilith, she refused his generous gift.

"I require no sacrifice. I ask only that you love her gently and break not her heart," Lilith whispered.

Lilith watched vigilantly from the shadows and made sure that Dagon was gentle and caring in his ways with Ensu. She could easily disguise herself through various glamours and did so not to intrude on their privacy but to protect Ensu if needed. Ensu was like a daughter to Lilith even though she was not born of her.

After a lengthy courtship, Ensu agreed to become the wife of Dagon. Lilith readied the sacred room which would witness their union. Shiamat spent three days ensuring the room would be perfect for the two lovers. The bed was stuffed with the purest cotton and the finest weaver in all of Sumeria. A woman named Jensir, had hand spun and wove the cotton sheets at Lilith's request. The finest beeswax candles were purchased to light the room, and the floor was covered with thousands of narcissus blooms.

Ensu was brought before Lilith to be made ready for her union with Dagon. Lilith sat Ensu down on the end of her bed and placed flowers in her hair while Shiamat rubbed a mixture of perfumed oils, beeswax, and powdered gold onto Ensu's skin. Lilith then braided Ensu's hair with strands of gold thread and accented her lips with rose-stain.

She presented Ensu with a white gown to wear. It was long, flowing and fastened with two small pins, one on each shoulder, which were shaped like small fish. The front of the gown draped in soft ripples across her breasts and had no back. Lilith watched as Ensu trembled as she nervously awaited the arrival of her lover. The sun was beginning to set and it would not be long before he arrived.

Shiamat left Ensu and Lilith alone as they waited for Dagon to arrive. Lilith blew gently on one of the candles. Every candle in the room began to blaze brightly. She laid he hand on Ensu's cheek and softly stroked her face.

"He will be gentle. I will see to it that he is. There is no pain in making love my child, only in what follows," Lilith whispered.

She walked slowly toward the door, stepped into the dark hall, and awaited Dagon as she left Ensu alone and trembling.

Dagon arrived dressed in a dark emerald green robe which nearly matched the color of Ensu's eyes. His eyes glowed an eerie shade of turquoise as he took Lilith in his arms to greet her. He stood nearly seven foot tall, and his skin shimmered in the light of the torches. He smiled softly at Lilith to ease her worries. Lilith drew her hands across his chest. Behind him stood his thirteen attendants, their arms filled with gifts for his new bride.

"Be gentle. She is nervous, and she is not yet a full Blood God. They are frail creatures, take care not to hurt her," Lilith whispered as she disappeared.

Ensu smiled softly as her love entered their sacred bedchamber. Dagon presented her with a large oval emerald as a token of his love for her and knelt before her.

Lilith stood in the shadows and watched as Dagon kissed Ensu gently and with reserve. He did not want her to be afraid. Dagon wrapped his arms around Ensu and tried to ease her fears. Lilith watched as Dagon touched Ensu with tenderness and caressed her softly as he edged her toward the center of their marriage bed. His love toward Ensu was evident in the way he touched her which caused Lilith to cry softly as she watched the two of them together. His love for Ensu was as deep as the sea. Dagon would never take her by force. Lilith was relieved.

As she left the two lovers alone in their embrace, Lilith waved her hand and the candles were extinguished, all but one. One flame burnt brightly, a solitary symbol of their love as they explored their passion.

Lilith sat alone of the steps of the temple and awaited the arrival of the sun. The moon shone brightly above her and the night air was crisp. It was the perfect night for lovers. She looked up at the large round moon above her and whispered, "thank you Inanna." The ring around the moon glowed brighter as though the Moon Goddess had heard Lilith's words of gratitude. Lilith laid down on the stairs of the temple and slept.

Lilith waited for three days for the lovers to emerge. It was evening on the third day when Ensu walked down the stairs and sat down by Lilith. Ensu looked up at the moon shining above them. Ensu was absolutely radiant. Lilith knew she was already with child.

"You are glowing, my child," Lilith whispered.

Ensu blushed and averted her eyes from Lilith as she smiled. She was embarrassed by the amount of time she had spent away from Lilith enjoying the act of love with her husband. She knew it had been many moons since

Lilith had been able to feel the touch of a man and did not want to make her sad.

"He wishes for me to stay with him until our child is born. Would you be angry with me if I did so?" Ensu asked.

"No, I shall not be angry. I only ask that I might be allowed to stay with you from time to time. I too worry about you Liadan. You have come to be the daughter I never had. I only desire to know you are safe and well," Lilith said as she touched Ensu's face.

"You have not called me that name in many years. Are you sad this night?"

"No my child, it is not sadness. I know now that your visions were true. The other five children were conceived last night and will be born during the alignment. I am filled with joy. For the first time in my life, I will have others who will be like me and who can receive my host. I have lingered between the world of men and the world of the Gods, never really belonging to either one. You cannot know the sorrow I have carried believing that I would always be the only one of my kind who was pure, uncorrupted, and immortal. Now I have hope, which is a strange emotion for me to embrace. I have you now. You are the first Blood God to grace Sumer and they will be my children, and I their creatress. I will no longer be the only pure source of the vampire race. Your child will share the virus with those who are worthy, and I shall never be alone again."

Ensu leaned against Lilith's shoulder and could feel her happiness. Lilith could not imagine her life without Ensu who had grown to be the daughter she longed so deeply for over the centuries.

Lilith made arrangements for Ensu to travel to Dagon's temple for the birth of their child. It was difficult for her to allow Ensu to be away for her for such a long period of time, but she understood Dagon's desire to have his bride with him and see his child enter this world. Lilith visited them in secret, disguised as one of Dagon's many wives. Though Dagon had many wives, he had but one consort, one he loved above all others; which was Ensu. As the child within her grew, Dagon grew more pleasant by the day. He longed to hold his daughter in his arms and whisper her name to the Gods of Dilmun.

Lilith longed for physical contact, but she could never again return to the Heavens. Though Enlil was cruel to her, Lilith still longed for him. She knew she could never love or embrace her beloved Enlil again. There was but one God left who could withstand her embrace, and he dwelled deep beneath the Earth.

Lilith announced she must leave for a period of four moons but would return before the child Ensu carried was born. Ensu was greatly saddened by Lilith's unexpected announcement and feared she had angered her mother.

"Have I displeased you?" Ensu asked as she cried.

"How could you displease me child? You are the Heavens and the Earth to me," Lilith whispered as she held Ensu in her arms as she cried.

"Why are you leaving me?"

"Your happiness has caused sadness to grow within my heart and this is no fault of yours. It has been many years since I have known the touch of a man or felt the warmth of his body beneath mine. I see the way Dagon looks at you and his heart wells with pride over his child growing within you. I know the peril the world faces when my heart fills with sadness and my world grows dark. I must leave you for a little while so that I may heal my darkness. I go only to see an old friend whom I have not seen in several thousand years so that I may know the embrace of another once more," Lilith said with sadness.

Lilith was not certain Nergal would see her. It had been nearly four thousand years since the Immortal War when she had given him her blood so that he might have an advantage over his father. She had seen in his blood memories that he desired her and loved her secretly from afar. Her blood had given Nergal unparalleled strength and granted him the ability to become a fearsome War God. He also accepted those who had died into his arms and cradled them at death until his mother, Ninlil, could once again give them life.

Lilith could not risk the humans seeing her take flight, so she waited until night had fallen to leave to find Nergal. She found him bloody and formidable as he stood above the battlefield below him. Lilith's feet touched down silently behind him, and she blew gently upon the back of his neck.

Nergal spun around quickly and brought down his magnificent mace. He stopped just short of striking Lilith. A wicked smile crossed her lips as she contemplated her fleeting thoughts of passion. Nergal swept her into his arms. He was astounded by her presence and awestruck by her beauty.

"Do you still desire me as you once did so long ago?" Lilith asked without hesitation.

Nergal gently placed Lilith on the ground next to him and leaned down over her. He closed his eyes as he drew her scent deep into his core. Nergal had forgotten how lovely she smelled. He towered over her as he questioned her.

"How is it you know this Lilith?" Nergal asked as he took her by her shoulders.

"By the memories you gave me in your blood when we once stood in Heaven together upon the battlefield of the Gods. Have you forgotten that day so easily?" Lilith asked as she batted her eyes at him.

"No one can forget you Lilith," Nergal said and smiled.

Lilith took his hand and walked with him across the battlefield. The carnage which lay before her made her sigh.

"Have you taken no wife in all these years?" Lilith asked.

"I have many consorts. They are not where my heart lies. My father bade me to marry and, by his force, one became my bride. She stays with me but half of the year. She is beautiful, but it is not her I love," Nergal said as he stopped to face Lilith.

"With whom does your heart lie Nergal? Tell me and I shall bring her to you," Lilith pleaded

"You," Nergal whispered.

As Lilith parted her lips to rebuke his words, Nergal kissed her. He drew the breath from Lilith's body, and she collapsed in his arms. When Lilith awoke she lay on a bed of crimson red in a crystal cavern surrounded by flowers. Nergal had left her untouched. He appeared before the end of the bed and lay down beside her. When Nergal leaned forward to kiss her again, Lilith placed a single finger to his lips.

"My kiss causes death. Please do not do this," she whispered.

"Have you forgotten what you gave me that day? I preside over life and death. You cannot kill me with a mere kiss," Nergal whispered as he drew Lilith's gown up her thigh and slid his hand under the small of her back.

"I can fulfill your desire if only you would let me," he said as he looked into her lavender eyes.

Lilith untied his leather applets, pulling them from his shoulders and then pulled the lacings from his shirt. She slid his shirt slowly over his shoulders and leaned in close to Nergal's chest. Lilith sighed as she sank her teeth into the flesh of his chest, and Nergal laid her down beneath him.

As the weight of his body bore down against hers, Lilith wrapped her legs around his waist, pulling him closer. It was the first time Lilith had allowed a God or a man to make love to her without her being in control. She allowed Nergal his place above her not in submission but because she knew he desired only to feel her body beneath him and desired to feel her embrace completely. He was compassionate as he touched her and made her complete. Tears streamed down Lilith's face, and Nergal grew concerned.

"Have I hurt you?" He asked.

Lilith could not answer him and instead allowed Nergal to drink her blood so he could see what she could not say. He saw the day that Atumn had held her down and taken her love from her without her consent. He saw the rage it caused within her, and how his own tender touch and caring manner had caused her to realize that he did not wish to dominate her. She knew Nergal only desired to feel her completely. Nergal's embrace had caused Lilith to let go the darkness that she had held in her heart.

Nergal rolled onto his back, pulled Lilith to him, and she smiled. She fell asleep as she lay on his chest with his arms around her.

Lilith stayed with Nergal for two moons before she realized she had to leave. He had become too intoxicated by her love and neglected his duties. The souls of those who died awaited his care. Lilith gathered her clothes, and with sadness, she bid Nergal farewell. He pleaded with her not to leave.

"Stay with me and I will spend eternity loving you," he whispered as he held her.

"You know I cannot. I must return to Eridu and wait for the birth of the chosen one. If I stay, you will remain lost in my love and continue to neglect those who need you the most. I will return to you one day. I promise," Lilith whispered as she pulled away from Nergal and slowly faded from his sight.

Lilith appeared in the temple and called to Shiamat who immediately came to her side.

"How is my lovely Ensu?"

"The child is near to the time of entering this world. Ensu is worried about the child which grows inside her and afraid of the birth. I reassured her you would return. Your arrival could not have come at a better time," Shiamat said as she lowered her head.

Lilith appeared inside Dagon's temple. She was greeted by Dagon's attendants, which took her directly to Ensu. Ensu paced the floor of her room nervously as she caressed her swollen stomach.

"Worry is not good for the child," Lilith said.

Ensu ran to Lilith and wrapped her arms around her as she began to cry.

"Something is wrong," Ensu whispered.

Lilith wiped the tears from Ensu's face and smiled at her as she held Ensu's face in her hands.

"She is fine. They both are. It is the heartbeat of two children you hear, not one. You should lie down. They will be here very soon."

Ensu had not been able to foresee the birth of her son; the male child which grew inside her, along with her daughter, was hidden from her sight. He would be the mirror image of his father Dagon, a boy who would grow to become a healer the same as his father Dagon and whose caring ways and nurturing touch could heal those around him. He would know the ways of herbs and the mysteries of the field. The male child within her would be nothing like his sister who possessed the same darkness as Lilith.

Lilith motioned to one of Ensu's attendants to come to her.

"Fetch Dagon, and quickly, for soon his children will be born," Lilith whispered.

Lilith watched Ensu closely as her breathing became more labored and difficult. The children inside her were taking a toll on her body. Though Ensu was a partial Blood God, her turning would not be complete till after the birth of her children. They grew within her from the seed of a God and this strengthened her in her Blood God form. Once the children were born, and Ensu drank from Lilith, her transformation would be complete. Lilith knew the birth would not be easy for her. Bearing the child of a God was taxing on the body and could endanger her.

Dagon appeared next to Lilith as Ensu screamed out in pain and collapsed as she held her stomach. Blood trickled from the corners of her eyes as she reached for her beloved Dagon. He swept her into his arms, carried her to their bed, and gently laid her down. Ensu continued to scream as the pain intensified until she lost consciousness.

Dagon was concerned for his beloved wife and tried to hide his fears from Lilith as he stroked Ensu's hair.

"I would not allow her to befall any danger," Lilith whispered as she slid her hand down Dagon's arm. "This birth will be difficult for her. She will need your love to help her through this and afterwards as well. I cannot imagine the sorrow she will have to face when the children are taken from her."

Dagon lowered his head. He knew that Ensu would never be the same after this day. The simple innocence she possessed was what had caused him to love her in the beginning. When the time came for the children to be taken from her that would all change.

"I assume she has been informed that the male child shall be raised within my temple with my loving hand to guide him," Dagon whispered.

"She has and I am grateful for your kind offer. He will grow to be a fine healer in your care and be responsible for his sister's resurrection many years from now. None of this could happen without your guidance. Ari is destined to become the Queen of our kind, and without Quinn, she would falter and die. I know you will be a devoted father to him," Lilith said with empathy in her voice.

The birth of Ari and Quinn was difficult and long. Day turned to night and by the next morning, Ari had taken her first breath, and within the hour, Quinn was born. Lilith held Quinn in her arms and studied his tiny features before she handed him back to his mother. She could feel the goodness within the child as he opened his eyes and looked up at her. His eyes were emerald green the same as his mother and his father. Ensu closed her eyes and continued to hold her child.

Shiamat sat quietly rocking Ari in her arms as Dagon held Ensu. It had been nearly four hours since the birth of her children when she had closed her eyes after seeing her son and yet she had not awoken. Dagon pulled her in close to his chest as he cradled her in his arms. He then did what no God was allowed to do, he slid a slice of the sacred golden apple between her lips. Dagon would endure any punishment that Enlil saw fit to dispense if it meant the mother of his children would live.

Lilith flew across the room in an attempt to stop him, but it was too late. The Dilmun Apple had already touched Ensu's lips. As Ensu drew her breath back into her, she arched her back away from Dagon and began to struggle.

"Give her your blood!" Dagon pleaded.

"It is forbidden. You know I cannot give her my blood now that you have broken the Law of the Gods! How could you give her a piece of the sacred apple? You have condemned us all," Lilith replied coldly.

"Please. She is the mother of my children and to her alone shall my heart belong. Do not allow her to die Lilith. Do not condemn me to the life of sorrow that you live. Do not condemn me to a life without love," Dagon whispered as he held Ensu tighter while her convulsions became stronger. Lilith knew if she stood by and did nothing, the woman whom she had grown to love as her own daughter would die.

Chapter Six
A Prophecy Written in Blood

Lilith tilted her head slightly to the right as she watched the child reach for his mother. The air of the room was thick and hot. It smelled of blood, sweat, and death. Lilith knew the scent which intoxicated her all too well. Yet, there was a sweetness to the stench of death that lingered in the room. She had smelled it once before when she was with Nergal in the Underworld. It was the perfume of Belet-Seri, the Scribe of the Earth. She collected the names of those who were about to enter the Underworld and presented them to Nergal before they died.

Lilith knew if she did not save Ensu now before Belet-Seri wrote in her name in blood upon the parchment within her hand that Ensu would be taken from her and this world.

"Leave this place Belet-Seri. She is not meant for you," Lilith whispered.

Lilith placed her lips to her wrist and pierced her flesh with her teeth. She held her wrist above Ensu's mouth watching as the blood ran across her lips and entered Ensu's mouth. Almost immediately, the convulsions ceased and Ensu began to breathe more steadily. Dagon pulled her to him and kissed her. Ensu slowly opened her eyes. They glowed an ominous deep green with a reflective shade of emerald. Ensu was now a Blood God. The child who had come to Lilith in the dead of night, who was born of God and Demi-Goddess, had eaten from the Immortal Tree which once belonged to Lilith and taken Lilith's blood. Her circle was now complete.

Quinn reached for his mother as Lilith held him, and she placed the child in his mother's arms then backed away. Lilith left the room and waited for the arrival of Enlil. It was not Enlil who came to see Lilith, but instead it was Ki. Ki embraced Lilith and kissed her softly on the cheek.

"I will grant Dagon this one indiscretion because of the injustice Enlil has done to you. Consider it my gift," Ki whispered and laughed softly. "Enlil is a juvenile and most inconsiderate. He knew not the love he could have had with you. You are fortunate to have found a life without my son."

Ki faded from Lilith's sight and left her alone in the corridor. It was the second time that Ki had interceded on Lilith's behalf. Though Lilith had not graced the Garden of the Gods in nearly a millennia, she knew that there were those who understood her plight. It gave Lilith a fleeting sense of satisfaction. Lilith paced in the corridor as she contemplated how to tell Ensu that the children would be placed with their new families in the morning. It was not safe to allow Ensu to bond too closely with either Ari or Quinn. She would be able to observe them from afar, but her contact needed to limited.

Lilith crept into the room and watched Ensu and Dagon as they held their newborns. The joy they felt overwhelmed her. She had never known the bliss of holding a child which had grown inside her. Lilith knew it was going to be very difficult for Ensu to let the children leave. Lilith longed to see Set. He was like a son to her, and she wished to look upon his face.

In the morning, Shiamat took Ari while Ensu slept and placed her with Adja. Adja was once a temple maiden and had been forbidden to have a child by temple law. She had just returned from a long absence of nearly a year. Shiamat and Adja could easily weave the tale of Sa-ari's birth. Adja looked at the small child whose auburn hair gently moved in the morning wind. The tiny child's eyes were the color of red sand as she looked up at her new mother.

Lilith sent Shiamat back to Ensu and bade her to keep watch over Ensu and Quinn while she journeyed to see Set. Lilith prayed silently that he would see her. She could not be sure what his reaction would be. She appeared in Set's temple just outside of Thebes. Egypt was still a child compared to Sumer. She saw Set standing before his altar as he prepared it for his worshippers.

"Set," Lilith whispered.

Set slowly raised his eyes to meet Lilith's. It was the first time she had seen him since she had arranged for him to be turned through magical rites. Lilith had no way of knowing if he held anger in his heart against her for taking him away from Ninti and Atumn even though he had offered himself willing to her and seemed pleased at the time of his transformation.

"Mother," Set whispered as he appeared next to Lilith and swept her into his arms.

"Mother?" Lilith asked.

"Who would be my Mother but the one who created me? Though I was not born from you, you gave me this life. We are all your children, and we are many," Set said and smiled.

He drew his hand through the air before Lilith's eyes and showed her the many Blood Borns who walked the Earth, children who had been born through Set from the gift of his blood and through her blood to him. Set lifted his hand before the image and it dissipated.

"How I have longed for the day when you would grace my palace and stand before me as the Supreme Mother of us all. Come, walk with me, and I shall show you your children," Set said as he laid his hand upon Lilith's shoulder.

Set took her to the many temples and allowed Lilith to view the Priests who now served them. The Egyptian mortals brought offerings to their Gods and gave their most beautiful daughters to serve them. Set had well over a hundred female mortals who pleasured him. As he walked through the temple with Lilith, they bowed at his feet and averted their eyes from him.

"They are most submissive mother. They behave as Ninti. You should be proud that you bow to no man and are strong-willed for these creatures have lost the ability to find their own way. They are weak like Ninti. I have yet to find a woman among the mortals who is the image of you, and until I do, I shall take no wife."

Set stepped into the sunlight, which was streaming through the atrium of the temple. The golden rays of the sun illuminated his black hair and it shined like black pearls. His skin shimmered under the rays of the sun from the scented oils that covered his skin. Lilith closed her eyes and drew his scent deep with her. He smelled of frankincense and dragon's blood palms. She could hear the soft rustling of his blood. Only one of her creations would mirror him in both strength and beauty and it was the daughter Ensu had just bore.

"With what honor do I owe the pleasure of your visit Mother?" Set asked as he commanded one of the slaves to kneel before him.

Lilith watched in silence as he tore the cotton shift from the woman's shoulder and buried his fangs deep within her flesh. She could feel the pleasure he took from the blood of the beautiful young temple maiden, and it caused Lilith to long for Nergal.

Set beckoned one of the temple Priests to come to him and kneel before his Mother. At first, Lilith refused knowing that once his blood entered her mouth it would cause sudden death, but then she succumbed to the growing bloodlust within her. Set watched Lilith as she drew her hands along the spine of the temple Priest and traced the lines of his muscular back. Lilith was a sensual being in every manner and simply touching the Priest gave her pleasure.

As Lilith stood behind him, she waited silently for the perfect moment to take the young Priest's blood. She brushed her lips against his skin before she bit him. Set watched as Lilith's deadly venom spread through the man's body as he writhed in pain on the temple floor below him and smiled. His Mother was still as lethal as ever.

"You have not lost your touch I see," Set said softly and began to laugh. His laughter echoed through the temple like mighty thunder. The humans dropped to the floor as they covered their ears.

"You still have not told me why you have graced me with your presence," Set whispered in his Mother's ear.

"A child was born this morn who will be very important to us my son, a female child who can withstand my embrace. She, along with five others, where born in the darkness of night when the eye of Sekhmet's Lion was high in the sky and the galaxy stood in line to witness their births. They will ensure the survival of our race. Ari will take her place among the Gods and become Queen of the Vampires," Lilith said with enticement in her voice.

"Blasphemy! You alone are the Queen to our race!" Set growled as his eyes grew dark and foreboding.

"My child, it is as you have said. I am the Mother to all of you, but I cannot also be your supreme regent as well. A Queen must have the conviction to be able to kill her subjects when they disobey her. I cannot lay judgment upon my own children and condemn them to death at my hand. Can you not see her importance? The vampire nation will grow strong and formidable under her guidance, which is why you must do this one task which I ask of you. You must put her prophecy to paper and hold it until the day Sephre is ready to know the truth. Only then can we set in motion the events which are yet to unfold," Lilith whispered.

Set bowed his head in reverence of Lilith's desires. She had created him and given him the life which he now enjoyed. He would obey her wishes.

"Today marks a special occasion, as I recall," Lilith whispered and then kissed Set upon his cheek.

Seth smiled deviously at Lilith and his eyes became a brilliant shade of red.

"Is there not a great feast this day in your honor?" Lilith asked.

"There is Mother and my heart is glad that you shall attend."

"I have brought you a gift to mark this day," Lilith replied.

Lilith slid her hand around her shoulders and called to her the serpent that once guarded her tree in the Garden of Dilmun.

"You have brought me a serpent mother? I have many serpents here already. I cannot accept from you the one who guarded your sacred tree as a gift."

The snake that was coiled around Lilith's shoulders raised his head and spoke with clarity.

"Child it is not I who am to be a gift to you for I would never leave your Mother's care. She has been good to me and loyal, for that alone, I will never leave her side. She has brought me to you so that I may grant you a gift which only I may give you," the serpent hissed.

Set leaned forward and looked into the serpent's blue eyes and the great serpent reared back before striking Set upon his upper arm. Set drew his sword, but Lilith bade him to re-sheath his blade.

Set looked down at the bite wound from the snake and watched as the venom wound its way around his bicep in a circular fashion then it stopped. A green and gold cobra emerged on his skin as though it was a tattoo but it had form and substance.

"You bear upon you now the mark of Supreme God my young Set. No man or God shall be able to speak false words to you, for if they do, the serpent upon your arm will strike them down before you. All Pharaohs who come to reign shall wear a band of the serpent upon their arm to honor you, including the young Scorpion King Sephre. I know there is much animosity between the two of you because Osiris went to his aid. Let not your anger lie with the man but with the God who dishonored you," the serpent whispered and then returned to his position around Lilith's shoulders .

Set slid his hand over the serpent that now adorned his arm and smiled at Lilith.

"You did not believe I would not honor the anniversary of your vampire birth did you?" Lilith said coyly and laughed. "Come now, and call your sages and scribes to pen what must be written."

Set called his finest scribes to record the prophecy as spoken by the serpent around Lilith's neck.

"On the day the stars in Heaven formed a line to the Gods, a child was born in Ur whose darkness could encompass the Earth. Her twin and her light, the male child, will one day bring her back from the depths of darkness. The male child will live within the confines of his father's house and be raised by the God who created them, and she will never know of his existence until after her transformation."

"The girl child, having been taken away from her mother, was raised by another. The love the woman gave her will allow her to learn and understand love in a way which she could not have learned had she stayed with her birth mother as the child is dark and compelled so to be. She will grow to be small in stature, much smaller than her five companions with whom she shall grow. The six children will learn the ways of the Sumerian Gods and will be trained in battle, the arts of sorcery, and divination. And so shall they be raised till the eve of the eighteenth year of their life and then they shall be committed to Lilith."

"The small one who was born of a God shall be the avatar of her people. She shall rise to fight a king whose ruthless and cruel ways subject his kingdom to torture and death. He will desire to possess her to build an army of Immortals over which he shall preside. Only the small one with darkness in her heart will be able to take down the mighty King and take him into herself and cause his death."

"A beneficent King, one of another land will create a race not unlike those of our own. They will be destined to have lives of great length and longevity with the gifts of prophecy. Born in the time of the rising of Nut against the stars, he will befriend the son of Set. He will love him as though the child of Set is his own son and make him a Prince. The son of Set shall live with him for many years and then take a wife of his own. All will be prosperous and well until the dark night of Anubis when another will come to the King. He will deceive him, making him believe he is one of his own heart. He will work his way to the inner sanctums of the kingdom and cause its' demise. His heart darker than the hearts of the lions of Sekhmet, he will feel no remorse for killing his own."

"Many years of darkness shall ensue. The children of the Dark Gods will feel as though there is no hope. They will go into hiding, living in a city of darkness underneath the city of men. Many years will pass before a woman shall be born, along with five companions. These children shall be born when Khonsu stands before Ra and causes the sky to turn black and Shes-nu, Smat, and Bau set low in the sky, and then they will then make their entrance to this world. They will be the first of their kind, unlike the ones before them. Their lives shall be never ending, consuming the blood of others. Their strength will be unequaled, their power formidable, and their gifts great. One among them is destined to be the Queen of the Undead. The small one who is born of a great Goddess shall be the ruin of the King and the savior of her nation. Her unusual beauty, and his desire to possess her gifts, will cause his downfall. When the eye of Sekhmet's lion is bright in the sky, she will strike the blow that will end his reign of tyranny."

"Darkness will swell and cover the land before she truly frees those who are her subjects. In darkness, she shall rest but not die. Her lust for blood will be formidable and her desire shall never wane. Carnage and blood soaked fields will lie before her, and she will revel in the glory of their blood."

"The small one and her companions from Ur shall rule the land until the time of darkness which rises in the first war of their kind. A war led by a King in a nation not his own, caused by his desire to possess the golden haired beauty who was once the consort of his father. His anger and sense of betrayal grew hatred within his heart toward the small one who gave shelter to the golden haired woman. He will take arms against the small one and turn her own kind against her. The casualties shall be great and her sorrow will be deep."

"The small one shall be triumphant, but it will not comfort her sorrow or her guilt. From her sorrow will rise the crowning achievement of her reign as Queen and her darkness shall subside."

"The reign of the small one shall unite the world of man and world of vampire in relative bliss till such a time as the worlds of the Gods again come to pay homage to the next great series of births. With this pending arrangement, a plague shall be unleashed and many mortals shall die. The world of the man shall shrink from their alliance with she who is Queen, and those she had created will seek the shadows and the cities which hide beneath the world of man as their sanctuary. Her darkness will be the difference between life and death and one among her race shall survive with her. They will give birth to the perfect race of vampires who shall repopulate the Earth once more."

The scribes wrote the words of the serpent as they flowed from him. When the serpent finished speaking, he took leave of Lilith and disappeared. Set bade the sages to illustrate the sacred text which was now in his possession. He placed it inside a small and ornate golden chest with carvings of scarab beetles and the wings of Isis to guard it.

"How is the young Sephre? Does he fair well?" Lilith asked.

"He is nearly aged to thirty now in mortal years, but he retains the look of his youth. Though it angered me that Sokara called to her the Scorpion Goddess and Osiris to save Sephre, I now can understand her decision to do so. I am desolation where Osiris is resurrection. She had to do what she believed would save her brother from certain death. Sephre has always been loyal to me. I am glad in my decision to give him a long life so that he may live to see the day when Ari gives him true immortality."

Lilith embraced Set and bid him farewell as she left him to attend the celebrations and feasts held in his honor. She knew what awaited her return to Ur. Lilith sensed it would not be pleasant.

Chapter Seven
The Tree of Woe

Lilith appeared outside Ensu's room only to be greeted by the henchmen who served Enlil. Thirty-six warriors stood before her armed with scimitars which glowed red in the dimly lit hall. Enlil appeared before Lilith and glared at her as he towered over her. Lilith crossed her arms as she sneered at her former love.

Shiamat appeared from Ensu's room next to Lilith and stepped in front of her. She was willing to give her life so that Lilith might escape.

"Shiamat, take Ensu back to the Temple of Inanna and prepare her for the Rites of Gestu. Ensure her contact with the child is limited. Ask Dagon for my forgiveness for I know not when I shall return," Lilith thought as she wrapped her arms around her faithful servant.

Shiamat spat in Enlil's face before Lilith caused her to fade from his sight. Enlil laughed at her brazenness in the face of a God.

"Lilith of Sumeria, you have betrayed me for the last time. You have given the mark of the serpent to another. You have coveted the serpent which belongs in the Garden of Dilmun without consent. You have stolen the golden apples of Inanna. You placed yourself as a Goddess among the Sumerian people. For your disrespect and blatant disobedience, I sentence you to contemplation upon the Tree of Woe," Enlil said.

Lilith smiled as it took all thirty-six of Enlil's guard to restrain her. She laughed as they bound her with golden thread woven by the Goddess Ereskigal to draw the souls of men from them at their death. When used upon a God or Goddess, it drew their strength from them.

Enlil slid his hands down Lilith's arms as the guards restrained her. He interlocked his hands around her back and pulled her closer to him until he could feel Lilith's body against his. A perversely wicked smile came to his lips.

"Crucify her," Enlil whispered as he backed away from Lilith.

The guards drug Lilith from Dagon's temple. She had no concern for her own welfare, only the welfare of Ensu and Ari was on her mind. She knew Shiamat would give her life to protect the child and her surrogate mother Adja.

The Tree of Woe sat alone in the vast and desolate wasteland that was once the Garden of Dilmun on Earth. Now a single tree lived within the center of the desert. It was used to punish the most vile and wicked mortals. The great tree towered only twenty foot above the desert floor. It was gnarled, twisted with a large split in the middle where both sections grew toward the Heavens. The Tree of Woe had no leaves for it fed upon the blood of those who were crucified there. Today the tree would bear host to Lilith and become her second home.

Lilith was placed inside the iron cage by Enlil, and four griffins drew her carriage. The thirty-six guards of Enlil surrounded the carriage as it was drawn deep into the desert. Lilith cried as she passed the Euphrates and saw the grave of her Prince. The roses of his tomb were in full bloom. The sweet scent of them caused her to cry. Enlil sat atop her iron cage and laughed at her tears.

"Weeping will not save you from my judgment Lilith. I have never fallen for your seductive ways and today shall be no different," Enlil said with little to no emotion.

Lilith turned and placed her face in her hands to hide it from Enlil. Her tears and her torment were none of his concern.

It took four hours to reach the Tree of Woe. It was now nearly dusk and the horizon was a mixture of soft reds and brisk oranges. Streaks of yellow danced across the sky and no clouds were visible. Lilith knew it would be a cold night in the desert.

Enlil personally removed her from the iron cage and tossed Lilith over his shoulder to carry her to the tree. He held her up by her waist as one of his guards drove the iron spikes through the bones of her wrists and then her feet. Lilith sighed as he drove the spikes through her flesh deep into the trunk of the tree and angered Enlil. Enlil then took two more spikes and drove them one by one through her shoulders. Lilith parted her lips and exhaled but never once cried out in pain or anguish. Enlil pulled a dagger from his vest and cut Lilith's gown from her body. He stood before her as the blood from her wounds trickled down her now naked body.

Enlil and his guards left Lilith alone on the Tree of Woe as night fell. It would be but the first of many nights Lilith would spend alone crucified upon the Tree of Woe. As darkness surrounded her, Lilith dreamt of the love she had once shared with Nergal and the promise that she had made to him. Lilith closed her eyes and went to sleep.

When Lilith awoke in the morning, she looked toward the Heavens. Would not one of them show her compassion?

As the heat of the day bore down upon Lilith, she closed her eyes and thought about her life. Should she have succumbed to the will of Atumn so that she could retain favor in Enlil's eyes? The memories of the day Atumn raped her came to the surface, and Lilith realized it was not wrong of her to caress and embrace her anger the way she had. No man, created by a God or not, had the right to take from a woman what she was not willing to give.

By the end of the first day of her judgment upon the Tree of Woe, Lilith's fair skin began to burn. Her soft and perfect milky white skin was now red and her lips were cracked and bleeding. She stood strong to her will. Lilith would not call Enlil to her for the apology he desired. She had done nothing wrong.

When dusk fell, Enlil appeared before her and circled the tree. He slipped a piece of passion fruit between her lips and gave her a small amount of water. The burning had finally subsided as the sun dropped below the horizon. Lilith's beautiful alabaster skin was covered with blisters which now bled and fed the Tree of Woe.

"Have you nothing you wish to say to me this night Lilith?" Enlil asked.

Lilith raised her head and spit in his face as he stood before her and smiled.

"I will die before I give you what you want," Lilith hissed.

Enlil laughed at how brazen Lilith was in the face of her own death and disappeared.

Each night Enlil would come to torture her and would stand before her as he asked Lilith the same question. Again, she would spit in his face and give him the same reply. By the end of the fourth day, Lilith lost consciousness as the Shinkar Vultures took roost in the tree.

Lilith's head hung down as the bird crept closer to her and began to tear the flesh from her shoulder. She held painfully still as she awoke to the pain of his beak pulling her flesh from the bone until the vulture was within her reach and then sank her teeth into the neck of the bird. The blood of the carrion feeder was repulsive and tasted of rotted flesh. It made Lilith sick as she fought to keep the blood down. She knew it would renew her and help her burns to heal.

Ki looked down from the heavens and cried as her first creation, the woman whom she had created with An from the primeval darkness, lingered in pain upon the Tree of Woe. Ki knew she could not interfere or go against her son so she pleaded with Inanna to help Lilith.

"Take to her your golden apples and feed them to her each night before Enlil arrives at her side," Ki begged.

"Why do you care for her so greatly? What is she to you Ki?" Inanna asked.

"She is my first born child. Long before the Heavens were created, long before the planets graced the nighttime sky, there was only darkness and from this darkness, I created Lilith. She has no memory of her creation. She only knows she lived in darkness with Ki and I until Enlil was born, and then he separated Heaven from Earth. Lilith knows not what she does. In her heart, she has only love and the desire to be loved. She loved Enlil above all others, but he rebuked her out of jealousy. He knows how much I love her. I knew not how to teach her how to truly love and created her without remorse. She does not understand the balance between a man and a woman, and that at times, we must bend to their will in a way where we do not lose our own. Lilith knows only her will and feels no remorse for her strength in being a woman. Please, I beg of you Inanna, do not let her linger in pain upon the Tree of Woe," Ki pleaded.

Inanna and none of the other Gods knew about Lilith's creation or that she was Ki's daughter. It was easy now for her to understand why Ki and An interceded on Lilith's behalf. They felt responsible for their daughter's actions and the lack of humility and guilt they instilled in her creation. Lilith was to be perfect and strong, a Goddess who would rival any God, but her power came from the blood she took from others and not from her strength in being a woman as they had planned.

"I will help her, but I will need your assistance. Enlil cannot catch me with her, or he will go directly to An. Call to Ningirama each night and bade him to weave a mist across the desert floor to conceal me as I go to her. May I ask what it was that Lilith did which angered Enlil?" Inanna asked.

"She favored Set above him. Enlil is still angry with Lilith over her abandoning Atumn and the death of Lahar and Ashnan. He is not one to forget so easily. I fear he will punish her all her days," Ki whispered.

"Even I would favor Set above Enlil for he is most beautiful and strong," Inanna said with longing in her voice.

"It is not that kind of favoritism Inanna. Set is a son to Lilith. She would never touch him in that manner. There is but one whom Lilith would now spend her life with but my son saw to him being forced to take a wife against his will to keep Lilith from having him," Ki said sadly.

"Nergal?" Inanna asked.

Ki nodded her head. Inanna and Ki knew together they could renew Lilith each day until they could find a way to free her.

That night Inanna appeared before Lilith as she hung on the Tree of Woe. The vultures had torn most the flesh from her body and her bones shown through the remaining flesh on her arms and legs. Though Lilith could not die in all actuality, she could feel pain. Inanna pulled her sickle shaped dagger from its sheath, sliced a piece of the apple, and slipped it between Lilith's lips. As the sacred nectar touched her tongue, the flesh on Lilith's body began to reform.

When Enlil came to Lilith that night, her body was restored to her. Her alabaster skin shone brightly in the light of the full moon.

"What manner of strange enchantment is this?" Enlil screamed.

"There is no enchantment here Enlil. I have only embraced my anger toward you and fulfilled a promise to myself. No man will ever control me and that includes you!" Lilith screamed.

Enlil stood only inches from her face as he touched her and attempted to seduce Lilith. He knew how deep her love for him ran. He implored whatever means were necessary to achieve what he desired. Lilith sighed as he touched her, but her will never caved. He could not take her blood from her in order to learn the truth without Lilith taking his first. He knew he could not force her to bite him. Even Enlil could no longer withstand her kiss. Lilith laughed, and it echoed across the Heavens above her.

"You have become as weak and insignificant as the humans you adore so much," Lilith whispered as she snickered at him.

In his anger and his rage toward Lilith's blatant disobedience, Enlil struck Lilith across the face. She continued to laugh at him. In his anger, he disappeared.

For the next thirty-six nights, Inanna came to Lilith and secretly gave her the golden apples and each night Enlil returned to her and grew more and more angry. He knew Lilith could not escape so long as the golden threads of Ereskigal bound her to the tree. Lilith could only pray that Set or Nergal would come for her.

Lilith did not know that Enlil had concealed the Tree of Woe from anyone who sought it. Even the God's could not find the tree except for Inanna. She took with her the sacred lions that Lilith had given her and used them to seek out Lilith's scent each night in the darkness.

Set searched for Lilith and could not find her. In his despair, he appeared in the crystal cavern of Nergal. Set knew his Mother cared for Nergal very deeply, and he prayed Nergal would help him. Set found Ereskigal sitting upon her thrown weaving her golden thread. She looked up at Set and smiled at him. He was very pleasing to her eyes.

"You search for my husband. He is not here," she said as she continued to weave.

"Tell me, beautiful Goddess, where I might find him and I will give you whatever you may ask of me," Set replied.

"He is not in my favor at this time. I care not where he is. He searches the Earth for his lost love, but he will never find her for I wove the thread which binds her to her prison," Ereskigal said smiling.

Set flew across the room in a rage that rivaled Lilith's anger and pinned Ereskigal beneath him with his dagger held to her throat.

"Careful Goddess, it is my Mother you speak of," Set hissed as the serpent upon his arm wound its way down his forearm toward Ereskigal.

No matter how hard she tried to struggle against Set, Ereskigal could not free herself from his grasp as the serpent crawled beneath her skin and forced her to tell him the truth.

"She is crucified upon the Tree of Woe," Ereskigal whispered as the serpent wove its way toward her heart.

"And where, Goddess, shall I find this Tree of Woe that you speak of?" Set asked her.

"In the desert waste land that was once the Garden of Dilmun," Ereskigal whispered as the serpent constricted around her heart.

Ereskigal succumbed to the venom of the serpent and died as Set held her down. Set placed his hand over her heart and allowed the serpent to crawl beneath his skin. Set smiled as the serpent wound its way back up his arm and once again became a gold and green tattoo.

"You have seen her heart, now show me the way," Set whispered to the serpent and closed his eyes. Set watched in horror as his mother hung from the Tree of Woe as her beautiful skin burnt beneath the searing heat of the sun. But the serpent could only show Set Lilith's location, he could not show him how to reach her.

Set sat in Ereskigal's throne and awaited the return of Nergal. He was the only one who could help him now. Set knew he could not find the wasteland alone. The location of the tree had been wiped from his memory when he accepted Lilith as his mother and betrayed his father. Set waited patiently as the next forty days passed. The body of Ereskigal still laid at his feet when Nergal returned.

Set was not expecting Nergal to return unannounced and was not prepared for Nergal's attack when he rushed him. The two Gods wrestled on the floor of the crystal cave until Nergal saw the serpent on Set's arm.

"Who gave this mark to you?" Nergal bellowed as he held Set down.

"My Mother, the Mother of my kind. She is the one you call Lilith," Set shouted.

Nergal released Set and then offered him his hand. Nergal stood over Ereskigal's lifeless body with little to no emotion.

"You grieve not for her. She was your wife. Was she not?" Set asked innocently.

"She is not with whom my heart lies. What did she say to you that caused such wrath?" Nergal asked as he continued to stare at her.

"She said she wove the thread which binds my Mother to the Tree of Woe. It was never my intention to kill her. I only desired for her to tell me the truth," Set said in an apologetic manner.

"Come then, we shall rescue your Mother and my Lilith," Nergal said as he handed Set a mace.

They appeared in the desert on Set's golden chariot and waited until they saw the heavens above them part. Nergal knew it was his father, Enlil, descending from the heavens to go to Lilith.

Enlil stood before Lilith and waited for the words he wished to hear. Just as the many nights before, Lilith spit in Enlil's face and laughed mercilessly. This time when he rose his hand to strike her, Nergal was there to intercede.

As Enlil drew back his hand to strike Lilith, Nergal grabbed his father's arm and forced him to the ground.

"Enough!" Nergal screamed. The anger in his voice rang through the Heavens above them like thunder and the ground beneath their feet trembled.

Set rushed to his Mother's aid and drew his dagger across his wrist. He allowed his blood to run along the golden threads which bound his mother to the tree, and they began to dissolve. Only the blood of her child could free Lilith from her bonds. Lilith had many children who were born from her blood who could have saved her, but it was Set who came to her in her darkest hour to free her.

"Have you not punished her enough father? She has quietly endured your mistreatment of her for two thousand years. Her only crime is that she loves you and would do anything to feel your warm embrace. When father will you finally set her free?"

Ki appeared behind Nergal and gently laid her hand on top of his.

"Let go of your father," Ki whispered and Nergal respectfully obeyed her. Nergal backed away from his father and lowered his head in the presence of Ki.

Ki watched as Set held Lilith in his arms and cried over the abuse she had endured. His tears healed her body as they fell and her badly burned skin began to fade. Nergal went to Lilith's side and brushed the hair from her face. He looked at her torn and weathered gown that lay at the foot of the tree.

"If he has touched you I will kill him," Nergal growled.

Ki struck Enlil with the back of her hand, causing Enlil to cower at her feet as the air around Ki began to glow an ominous shade of red.

"I have endured your behavior because you are my son. You are no longer in my favor Enlil. Touch Lilith again and I will involve An, which I do not believe you wish me to do. Am I understood?"

Ki snapped her fingers and Enlil disappeared. She knelt next to Lilith and touched her daughter's hair.

"Take her to your home Nergal and keep her close to your heart. I will send others to tend to the souls of those who have come to rest in your care so that you may help her to mend," Ki said as a single tear rolled down her cheek.

"And you, you are the young God Set. Lilith is fortunate to have a son so obedient and loving. I am grateful for your love for her and the depth of your caring. Even though Lilith is not your true Mother, she is the one who created you. She loves you very deeply."

Ki disappeared. Set carried his Mother to his golden chariot, and Nergal then held Lilith in his arms as Set drove his chariot across the desert to Nergal's home.

"I knew you would come for me," Lilith whispered as she looked at her son. "I knew if Set could not find me, then it would be you who would rescue me," Lilith said as she laid her head against Nergal's broad shoulder.

Lilith did not speak as they drove across the desert to the entrance to the Underworld. Nergal swept Lilith into his arms gently as he carried her to the bed of crimson and tenderly laid her down. Both Set and Nergal watched silently as Lilith cried herself to sleep. Nergal was still angry and wondered what Enlil had done to Lilith as she hung upon the Tree of Woe.

Nergal sat in his throne while Set made himself comfortable in the corner of the room. He laid his head upon his knees as he kept a watchful eye over his Mother. He understood now the rage that she had held in her heart for so long. As his black feathered wings unfolded, Set wrapped them around himself and fell asleep.

Nergal keep vigil over Lilith. Every so often she would stir slightly and cry out in her sleep. Each time she did, Nergal would lean over her and lay his hand on her shoulder so Lilith would know she was safe.

Lilith slept for three days before she finally rose from Nergal's bed. She was silent as she watched her son sleeping. His breath softly moved the feathers of his wings which were still wrapped around him like a protective cocoon. She realized how exhausting his search for her had been. Set smiled softly in his sleep at his Mother's touch.

Nergal rose from his throne, wrapping his robe around Lilith and edged her back toward his bed. Lilith slid beneath the camel skin's that covered Nergal's crimson bed. Nergal laid down next to her. He pulled the covers over her shoulders. Nergal could not bear to see her in such pain, but he also knew that Lilith would speak no angry words against his father, nor would he ever know what truly happened to Lilith under Enlil's watch.

"What have I done to make you love me this way?" Lilith asked.

"Why would you ask me such a question?" Nergal said with a puzzled look.

"I have done nothing to warrant your love. I am undeserving," Lilith whispered.

Nergal tucked her hair behind her ear as he looked into her eyes.

"Why must you punish yourself this way?" Nergal asked. "You are just as worthy as any Goddess or any mortal woman to know love and be loved."

Lilith closed her eyes and sighed as she pressed her face into Nergal's hand.

"Stay with me Lilith, if only for a little while longer," Nergal whispered.

"I shall stay as long as time permits," Lilith replied as her thoughts began to wander. She moved closer to Nergal so she could feel him next to her.

Nergal pulled her closer to him and whispered, "With you my heart shall always lie, Lilith of Sumeria."

"And mine shall with you," Lilith whispered as she drifted off to sleep.

Lilith knew her bliss would not last. Though in her heart she longed to stay with Nergal for all eternity, Lilith knew she would eventually have to return to Ur.

Chapter Eight
The Creation of Ari

Lilith sat quietly the next morning as she watched Set sleeping while she waited for him to wake. She knew Set needed to return to Egypt quickly. Sephre was due to leave Egypt under the care of King Bashura early the next morning. Set needed to ensure both the true and false prophecy about Ari left Egypt with them. Though it broke Lilith's heart to bid Set farewell, she did so for the good of all vampires.

Set kissed Lilith softly on her cheek before he disappeared. Lilith could feel the downdraft from his wings as he flew from the crystal cavern to his awaiting chariot. She knew it would be many years before she would see him again.

Lilith remained in the great crystal cave with Nergal for nearly seventeen years. She aided Nergal in his care of the souls who awaited their judgment and was a loving consort. Lilith traveled to the world of man every so often to see Shiamat and check on Ari, but she would always return. Lilith knew she would soon have to return to the mortal world to aid in her greatest creation. She also knew that once she set foot on the sands of the Sumerian Desert, it would be over six thousand years before she could return to her loving Nergal or stay with him the way she now desired.

The next year passed quickly in the Underworld with Nergal. Lilith had at last been able to not only feel true love but also give the same in return. Nergal loved Lilith without bounds and in a completely selfless manner with no motive other than wanting Lilith to be happy.

Enlil had not forgotten about Lilith. He patiently waited for Lilith to return to Sumeria. If he could not keep her under his watchful eye, then he would use her most prized possession to get to her. Enlil would manipulate Ari's destiny to make Lilith miserable.

Lilith bid Nergal a tearful farewell and arrived in Ur the morning before the transformation of Ari and her companions was due to take place. Shiamat could not believe her eyes as Lilith stood before her. She noticed that Lilith was different. She was even more beautiful and more radiant than she had been before, and it was the kind of beauty which radiated from deep inside Lilith. Lilith's anger had been replaced by something else. Shiamat wondered what had happened on the Tree of Woe to change Lilith.

"My friend, it pleases me to see you. It has been far too long since you have graced me with your presence. The children have grown strong in your absence, Lilith. Ari and her companions anxiously await your embrace," Shiamat thought as she held Lilith tightly.

"I have longed to see you as well. I am sorry my visits had to be so infrequent. I have healed my heart, Shiamat, through the loving touch of Nergal," Lilith said as she continued to hold her Priestess.

Lilith had learned to love without guilt and without pain. She had allowed another into her heart and learned to accept love. It was a gift that Inanna and Ki bestowed upon Lilith for the countless years Enlil had mistreated her. Even Lilith's anger toward the humans had softened in her absence. Though she would always view them as weak, she no longer despised them because Enlil loved them.

"Is the Temple at Eridu ready for their arrival?" Lilith asked.

"Yes, and today shall be their day to feast and enjoy the last pleasures of their mortal world. Ensu insisted that we send laced wine for them to drink before the journey to

Eridu. Your temple has been made ready for them. All we need to do now is to wait for nightfall," Shiamat said as she bowed to Lilith.

Lilith floated gracefully down the corridor to Dagon and Ensu's room and knocked softly. When Ensu opened the door she fainted, and Lilith barely caught her in her arms. Lilith held Ensu in her arms till she awoke.

"I did not believe it was you. You have been gone for so long," Ensu whispered.

"I am whole now my child. I can now be the Mother I was destined to be. Tell me, how is your daughter and your son?" Lilith asked.

"Quinn has grown into a fine young man. He stays with his father. I do not see him as often as I would like. It is better this way, even though it causes me great pain. Ari is as willful and disobedient as ever. Adja loved Ari above all others. Perhaps this led to her willful behavior since Adja indulged her every whim. Ari will bond with Drake just as we have foreseen," Ensu said calmly.

Lilith knew the sorrow which was hidden in Ensu's voice. Lilith loved both Set and Ensu, and it was difficult for her to be away from them. She could only imagine how hard it would be to spend your life silently observing them and never being able to let them know who you really were.

Lilith wrapped her arms Ensu and held her.

"Your sorrow will soon end. In a few days you will be able to tell Ari the truth, and this will lighten your heart," Lilith said as she held Ensu tightly.

"I will leave you to make the necessary preparations for their arrival. I must speak with Shiamat," Lilith said and disappeared.

Lilith appeared behind Shiamat as she readied the caravan to send to Ur.

"Shiamat, has the false prophecy been delivered to Sephre as well as the true one?" Lilith asked.

"Yes. They have been delivered. Sephre has placed the true prophecy in the care of his sister, Sokara, and King Bashura has been made aware of the plan."

Lilith went to the hall to oversee the last details of the preparations for the arrival of Ari and her companions. Every minute detail needed to be flawless. Precautions needed to be taken to ensure the safety of the Priestess' and Priests within the Temple. They would be the first vampires ever created solely by Lilith, the first perfect vampires to mirror her in every manner possible. Though Blood Borns had been created through sacred rites, they were born from a diluted form of Lilith's blood. The Blood Borns did not possess the host of Lilith like Ari and her friends soon would.

Set was able to withstand Lilith's embrace only because he was the son of Atumn who was created by Enlil. But even Set could not withstand Lilith's kiss, or the pure infection within her blood. Set was a Blood Born just the same as the ones Lilith allowed him to create. He was allowed, through the grace of his mother, to infect a small group of others who were loyal to King Bashura. The King would in turn invoke Lilith the same as he had witnessed. It was all part of the elaborate plan which Lilith wove without their knowledge.

Lilith had waited patiently for this day to come for many reasons. Enlil had put his creation, the human race, above all others including the other Gods and Lilith. When they could not care for themselves, it was Lilith who cared for them and showed them compassion. Lilith now had the power to change Enlil's most prized possession, his frail and weak humans, into a race worthy of the Gods. They would be Lilith's crowning creation, and they would be flawless. With Ari as their supreme regent, Lilith would not need to worry that what had happened on the original home of the Gods would happen again.

Lilith called to Set to arrange the transport of Ari, Drake, Annara, Anju, Drusil, and Souri to Eridu. He arrived only moments after Lilith called to him. They walked through the Ziggurat together. Lilith took Set to the room where Ari would leave her humanity behind and become their Queen.

The room was draped in dark crimson and purple fabric with gold edging. The altar had a finely woven purple cloth covering it that was embroidered with a gold dragon in the center that was flanked by two griffins. Lilith and Set watched Ensu carefully place each chalice on the altar along with a golden dagger. The blade of the dagger was engraved with the image of two lions, and the grip was wrapped in soft, white camel skin.

Lilith and Set left Ensu alone to finish the final preparations. Lilith waited patiently as Set drove the caravan to Ur. The caravan was draped in the same crimson and gold fabric as the altar room. Set touched each one of them as they boarded the caravan just as Lilith had instructed. The effects of his touch would keep them in a comprised state until they received Lilith's gift.

Lilith walked the corridors of the Ziggurat as she awaited Ari's arrival. She paused at the room that awaited Ari and opened the door. As she stood in the doorway, Lilith admired the fine suit of Sumerian Armor that silently awaited Ari's arrival.

Lilith watched through Set's eyes as he transported them to Eridu. The streets of Ur where empty and the mighty city appeared abandoned. Set had stolen the six of them away in the darkness of the night.

Much preparation had gone into the pending arrival of Ari and her friends. Kings from each region of Sumeria had sent their well wishes and gifts to welcome them. They would become the guardians of Sumeria. Each room was filled with the riches of Sumeria's Kings. Chests filled with gold and jewels lined the wall of the room with their contents spilling out onto the floor.

In the center of the each room stood a suit of Sumerian Armor that Nergal had sent to honor those who would become Lilith's children. Six sets of armor stood awaiting them as a gift. He had begun crafting the armor when Lilith was recovering from her time upon the Tree of Woe. The armor was Nergal's gift to Lilith in honor of her love.

Nergal had painstakingly crafted each set of armor for those who would become the children of Lilith. She had watched him sew each layer of leather over the next until it was perfect. The dark sunset color of the leather glowed in the candlelight. It was the perfect gift for the woman who was about to become the perfect vampire. Lilith smiled as she closed the door and thought about her love and the day they would be re-united.

Lilith stood in the shadows as she awaited their arrival. Her eyes flashed from lavender to dark purple as she waited nervously. Lilith knew the task that lied ahead of her would not be an easy one. Each God of Sumeria possessed a host. Lilith was no different. Though she had willingly descended to Earth to care for Enlil's humans, she had not relinquished her host. An and Ki could not bear to take from Lilith what gave her immortality and her darkness. It was what made Lilith complete. She was essentially the same powerful Goddess she was the day they created her. The separation and division of a host could be a dangerous endeavor. Lilith prayed silently all would proceed as she had planned.

The caravan arrived and Set guided them into the Ziggurat. Ensu greeted them and led them to their rooms. Lilith hid in the shadows and watched as Ari surveyed the room. As Ari circled the armor in the center of the room and drew hand across it, Lilith was filled with joy at Ari's pleasure from Nergal's gift. Lilith faded from the shadows and appeared next to Ensu in the Great Hall.

"She has grown into a beautiful woman who is the perfect image of both her parents," Lilith whispered as she stepped into the shadows as Ari and her companions entered the Great Hall.

Ensu began the ceremony to invoke Lilith. It was all part of the plan the two of them had devised many years prior. Lilith desired to keep the extent of her involvement in their lives secret. Though she would be close to them all their lives, she preferred to observe them without their knowledge. Ensu chanted in her native tongue and called forth the Mother of all vampires. Lilith appeared on the altar before Ari and took the dagger from Ensu's hand. She smiled as she drew the dagger deep across her wrist and filled the chalices with her blood.

Lilith drew in a deep breath as the separation of her host began. The pain of the separation caused Lilith to cry out in pain and a great wind rushed through the hall. Ensu's hair tangled around her face and partially obscured her view of Lilith. She watched as Lilith dropped to her knees and slammed her hand into the altar causing the corner to crumble beneath her strength. The separation of Lilith's host had begun.

Lilith's eyes became blood red as a piece of her host slid between her lips into each chalice one by one. She inhaled sharply and the wind within the great hall ceased and created an eerie silence before she disappeared.

Lilith watched through Ensu's eyes as Ari lifted the chalice to her lips and accepted her immortality. The chalice fell from Ari's hand and dropped to the stone floor beneath her. Lilith knew the transformation would be painful for them, but she also knew that these six young men and women could withstand what they faced. The alignment they were born under had made their blood unique, so unique that they were the only mortals who could withstand Lilith's deadly blood and her host.

As Lilith watched her blood course through Ari's body, she could feel the precise moment when her host bonded to Ari. The force and pain of the bond thrust Ari forward, and she slammed her hands into the stone floor causing the stones to crumble beneath her newfound strength.

Ari stood and watched Annara and Drusil as they were transformed by Lilith's blood. She closed her eyes and lifted her face toward the Heavens as she drew in her first breath as vampire. Lilith watched the euphoric pleasure of her new senses wash over Ari as she realized she could smell the blood of the others within the room, and the blood of those Ensu had brought for them to feast upon. Lilith drew her hand through the air and filled Ari with the knowledge of how to exist as a vampire and Ari smiled.

Ari stood silently as she watched the humans be released into the hall to meet their deaths. Ensu closed the door behind her and locked the humans inside the Great Hall to face their demise. Ari took pleasure from watching Annara and Drusil work in tandem, tearing the humans apart limb from limb in the fury in which they fed. The bond they shared as twins increased the fury with which they killed their victims, and they shared the power and feeling between them.

Lilith swooned in the aftermath of the blood they shed together. The room filled with the delicious scent from the blood of the humans. She could feel Drake's concern for Ari, and Lilith knew that Ari could now feel the extent of his love for her. Ari watched as Drake called them to him. He was not cruel or merciless in the manner in which he took their lives from them. The desire to feed within Ari continued to grow until she could no longer control herself.

Ari's darkness was unleashed and Lilith sighed. Ari's creation was now complete.

Lilith knew that Ari would do whatever was necessary to protect her family, even if it meant killing her own kind, which was the one task Lilith could not do. They were all her children, the vampires who soon would grace the Earth. Lilith understood the darkness within Ari would be difficult for her to control, but it would be the difference between the legion of vampires Ari was about to create being able to be controlled and the complete annihilation of the human race.

She tilted her head slightly as she watched Ari pull the blood soaked hair from her face and embrace her family. This night Ari would embrace Drake just as Lilith had foreseen and together they would become an unstoppable force.

Lilith went to Ensu who sat quietly upon the stairs of the Ziggurat. She sat next to Ensu and took her hand in hers.

"It is done my child. All six have survived just as we foresaw, just as you foresaw so many years ago."

Lilith could feel Ensu's relief as she heard Lilith speak the words that her daughter had survived the painful transformation.

"I will leave you to tend to them in the morning. I must go to Set and speak to him about King Ashurhassan. I have foreseen what his plans are for your daughter," Lilith said as she stood.

"The King?" Ensu asked.

"Yes. I am disheartened that he would use his power in such a manner. His only love is power and he desires to be the most powerful King to grace the soil of Sumeria. It was my hope that when Bashura enlisted my aid to create Ashurhassan as a Blood Born he would embrace my will. He is consumed with bloodlust only and will do whatever is necessary to possess your daughter. He desires to use Ari to create an invincible army and for her to be his breeder," Lilith said mournfully. "Annara is strong in her gifts of prophecy. She will foresee his intentions and inform the others. Allow her to be the one who tells them what his desires truly are. You must not reveal that you know anything about the King's plan. It is imperative for Ari to take her place as Queen. This will enable her to embrace her title with more ease."

Ensu nodded and remained silent as Lilith swept her cape around her and disappeared. It had been many years since she had stood inside the Temple of Set. The walls were more elaborately decorated than that of her last visit to Egypt. Pillars of malachite and lapis adorned the hall that led to the inner sanctuary that held Set's Priests, brilliantly painted figures told the story of Set's life and how he was born from an Immortal.

Lilith drug her hand along the wall and touched the paintings and hieroglyphs about her son. She began to hum softly and the attendants within Set's temple bowed at her feet as she passed. She stopped momentarily to observe them as they swayed to the sound of her soft humming. Lilith stopped and touched the hair of the young Priest who knelt before her.

"So easily influenced, so easy to control," she whispered as she continued down the length of the corridor that led to Set's private sanctuary.

Set was reclined on a long rolled back divan with four slave girls attending him. Three of the women fanned him with large palm frawns as the fourth girl sat on his lap with her arms around Set. His face was buried in the hair of the slave girl as he whispered softly to her. The young woman snickered shyly at the implication of what he was saying to her. Lilith stood with her arms crossed as she watched Set manipulate the beautiful young girl to bend to his every whim. Set looked up to see Lilith patiently waiting for him to notice her. He kept his arms wrapped around the young woman with whom he was obviously enamored.

"Is she not the most beautiful creature your eyes have ever beheld, Mother?" Set asked Lilith as he drew his index finger down the young woman's slender arm.

"Is she who entertains your current whim?" Lilith asked Set.

"Her name is Astarte. She heralds from the Syrian Desert. I desire to make her mine," Set whispered and as he did, Astarte was easily influenced by his words and began to sigh at his touch.

"She is beautiful, but I sense there is more to her than just her beauty."

Set gave his Mother a quick angry glance. Lilith knew all. There was not any occurrence that could be kept from her sight, especially when it involved one of her immortal children.

"I am at war with Osiris. He is petty and believes the Earth should weep at his feet. He desired Astarte, so I took her from him. He wished to make her a fertility Goddess in the eyes of my people. Anyone who is even remotely observant can easily see she is meant for war." Set wrapped his arms around Astarte and pulled her closer to him.

"Set!" Lilith screamed.

Set whispered into Astarte's ear. She immediately stood and bowed to him and then bowed to Lilith.

"I have much I need to discuss with you. Ari's transformation is complete, but we have other issues we must deal with immediately. Now is not the time for pleasurable indulgences," Lilith said sternly as she motioned for Set to follow her. "Ashurhassan is proving to be a difficulty. We must ensure that Hammurabi will support us in this undertaking. I want you to go to him on my behalf and approach him about the city beneath his lovely Babel. We must have a place for Sephre and

Anephret to take refuge. I must know that Hammurabi will not betray the location of the city of Capurincus. Ensu will travel soon to enlist his aid to strengthen Ari even further. You must do this for me Set and do so without argument."

Lilith's voice was soft and comforting as she used it to soothe Set into doing what she wanted. She knew that Set secretly held jealous feelings toward Ari even though he tried not to harbor them. Set loved Lilith above all others. It saddened him that Lilith now held another in higher regard than him. She was his creatress, his Mother, and his reason for being.

Lilith's movement was fluid and entrancing as she walked with Set. Her grace and beauty flowed from her as she walked. She did not wish for her son to hold anger in his heart toward Ari. Ari, after all, was her child too.

"I do not love you any less my child. There is room within my heart for me to love all my children, but you will always be the first and most important to me. You gave yourself to me and honored me as your Mother. You took from me my blood and survived. You were my first creation Set, and I love you no less because I have created her," Lilith thought as she took Set's hand.

When Lilith touched Set, she realized that it was not as much anger or jealousy he held in his heart but sadness. He would no longer be her greatest creation. Ari possessed the host of his Mother, a feat which Set could never do. Set had withstood Lilith, but he was but a Blood Born. He was created through mystical means the same as Set had used Lilith's blood to create Sephre. Lilith stopped Set, laid her hands on his face and cradled it.

"You will always be perfection in my eyes, and I will always love you," Lilith whispered and kissed her son.

Set lowered his eyes. He was ashamed of the way he was feeling. He was strong and virile, a God in his own right. Jealousy was not becoming of him.

"Will Hammurabi agree to an audience with me Mother?" Set asked.

"He will see you. Hammurabi owes both Ensu and I many favors. He will agree to the terms with which I need him to abide. Every seven years a young man among the Sumerians is chosen to be the representative of Dagon. He is given part of Dagon's host, represents him on Earth as the God himself and becomes Dagon to his followers. It will not be long before his representative will be sacrificed, and the ashes of his heart will be stored for the next incarnation. Ari must consume the ashes in order to defeat Ashurhassan."

"Where is Dagon?" Set asked innocently.

"He resides within his Temple at Ur, but he will travel to his temple at Lagash for the ceremonies. He stays within the shadows and allows his representative his glory. Dagon is fiercely handsome and yet somewhat startling in his appearance. He towers above the humans at nearly seven feet tall. The only one I have ever seen who does not cower in his presence is Ensu. She has no fear of him, only love. With the host of two Gods within her, Ari will be unstoppable. I am sure you can now see why it is imperative that this happens. Though I had great hopes for Ashurhassan when Bashura came to me and asked for my grace to invoke my presence, he is dangerous and unruly. He cannot be controlled and will cause the downfall of our kind if Ari does not kill him. I cared a great deal for King Bashura. He was a good man. I know your Sephre is deeply saddened and angered by his death," Lilith said calmly.

"I will leave this evening if it pleases you. You have worked too hard to bring the vampire race into the world. I will not have one wayward King bring it all down around your feet," Set said with an angry tone.

"There will always be those who cannot blend their mortal ways seamlessly with our venom. That is why there is Ari. She will lay judgment and rule them firmly. They will fear her and what she will become."

Lilith thought about the dark times that were yet to come and how painful it would be for her to not be able to intercede. She knew that Drake's love, along with his compassion and his understanding of Ari's dark nature, would be what would ultimately save her from her own darkness. Lilith disappeared and left Set standing alone on the stairs of his Temple as Astarte appeared and wrapped her arms around him.

Chapter Nine
Shadows

Lilith thought long and hard about her involvement with Ari and the members of her new family. Though it would be extremely difficult, Lilith knew she could not interfere directly. She would have to allow the future to unfold however the Gods saw fit, or better yet, she would allow others to intercede on her behalf.

Lilith silently pondered if Enlil was angered by her newfound power over his prized creations. It made her smile as she walked along the banks of the Euphrates as she contemplated how angry it would cause him to grow when he realized what she had done. Perhaps satisfaction was finally within her grasp.

Inanna appeared next to Lilith as she walked.

"You should not toy with him Lilith. We cannot always intercede on your behalf," Inanna said calmly.

"He no longer matters to me. I have my children to care for, an entire race of vampires who emulate me. Why should I care what he thinks or if he wants to pout like a spoiled child?" Lilith asked.

"You know his temper is formidable and what he capable of doing when he is angered, especially when it involves you. The humans have begun to forget An and Ki and have made Enlil their supreme ruler," Inanna replied.

Lilith stopped and turned to face Inanna as she stopped speaking. She scrutinized Inanna's expression as she looked at her. Lilith knew Inanna was speaking the truth.

"And An and Ki would allow this after everything he has done?"

"It is time for An and Ki to become the supreme rulers of the Gods and their realm. There must be one for the humans to honor as their own God. Who better than their own son to fulfill this need? Would you not place Set in the same position if the opportunity arose?" Inanna asked as she began to walk again.

"There is no comparison between Enlil and my Set. Set is an obedient son and honors me as his Mother above all others. Enlil honors only himself. He is full of conceit and pride," Lilith said scornfully.

"And you are not? You, Lilith, who once lived among the Gods, became the wife of Atumn because Enlil bade you to do so. You, who would not lie beneath Atumn and submit to his will, have the audacity to say that Enlil is full of pride?" Inanna said laughing.

Lilith grabbed Inanna by her arm and forced her to the ground at her feet. She leaned over Inanna and her eyes glowed brilliant red. Lilith turned Inanna's arm until she could see the pain upon her face.

"It had nothing to do with pride! He took from me by force what I was unwilling to give! No man, created by a God or not, should have that kind of power over a woman!" Lilith screamed. "Go back to him and tell him I will never submit to his will! I will make his humans suffer for what he has done to me!"

Lilith pushed Inanna, and Inanna fell onto her side. Inanna raised her arm to shield herself from Lilith's rage.

"Lilith, please, do you not remember it was I who stopped your suffering upon the Tree of Woe? I did not know that Atumn raped you. Enlil failed to mention that detail. I beg your forgiveness," Inanna said as she lowered her eyes.

"Enlil is like the trickster Enuki. His words are coy and his breath full of lies. You would be wise to distance yourself from him Inanna. The humans hold you in high regard. One day this will anger Enlil. The same fate that befell me could befall you as well. I would wade the waters carefully Inanna. I do not wish upon you the fate which Enlil gave me," Lilith said as she offered Inanna her hand. "I will always be eternally grateful for you kindness while I was bound to the Tree of Woe. I will never forget what you have done for me."

Lilith's tone was sincere. Inanna knew she meant every word she had said, but she still could not help herself from fearing for Lilith's safety. She knew Enlil would use any means at his disposal to make Lilith miserable. Enlil was not quick to forget any indiscretion against him, no matter how many millennia had passed.

"Guard well your creation Ari. He will do whatever is within his power to take her from you just to anger you," Inanna whispered as she spread her luminous white wings and then took flight.

As Lilith continued to walk along the Euphrates, she wondered if Enlil was behind the corruption of King Ashurhassan. It could very well be that he was behind the death of Bashura as well. Lilith knew in her heart that Enlil had struck a bargain with Ashurhassan. She just did not know what it was that he had promised him.

Lilith stopped to pluck a lily from the edge of the water. The flowers had been named for her by the humans who were once in her care. The beautiful white flower with its bright red pistils reminded her of how much she had once loved the humans who had lived within her beautiful garden Dilmun. The humans who were descended from those who once lived in her garden would continue to be the recipients of her love. Only those descended from Enlil's creations who were loyal to him would reap the wrath of Lilith. Lilith longed to return to the Underworld and leave the world of mortals behind. She wished to hold Nergal in her arms and reclaim the happiness she once had as her anger began to grow once more.

Lilith continued to watch Ari from the shadows as her power and gifts began to develop. Her traits were much the same as Lilith's. She could blend into her surroundings with little effort, and her ability to control others was impressive. Ari could smell the blood of the humans just the same as Lilith, and it pleased Lilith that Ari's senses were nearly as strong as hers. Ari could perceive the power within other vampires and knew how their powers would benefit her. It would only be a matter of time before Ari would learn how to take their power from them and make it her own. Ensu had given birth to the perfect child, and Lilith had made her the perfect vampire.

Lilith took pleasure in walking along the Euphrates each morning and contemplating what her next course of action should be. As Lilith continued her slow stride along the river, she realized a small detail had eluded her. She had been so consumed with creating Ari, and her rage against Enlil, Lilith had never congratulated Shiamat on the birth of her sons. Shiamat had born two fine sons in her absence when she had remained with Nergal to heal, and Shiamat had named her sons Zaid and Lugal. Lilith did not know who the father was but knew that they gave Shiamat great joy. Shiamat had left them in the care of their father and visited them when she was able to travel to them. Zaid would be nearing the twentieth anniversary of his birth soon. Lilith felt remorse for not remembering the most momentous day of her loyal friend's life.

Lilith's eyes glazed over as she saw the day of their conception replay before her eyes. Shiamat had lain with King Ashurhassan and become one of his many consorts. She had born his first two sons. How could this fact remain hidden from her eyes?

"Enlil," Lilith said as she began to fume with anger. "You have interfered for the last time!"

Lilith screamed at the Heavens above her. She knew that somewhere Enlil was content in the deception he had created and the anger it had caused in Lilith.

"If this is the manner in which you desire to play, then I shall even the odds," Lilith whispered.

She knew how conceited Ashurhassan was and that his children with Shiamat were Half Bloods, half human and half vampire with the power of Lilith coursing through their veins. She would call to her son Set and have him finish their transformation and allow them to become Blood Borns. Lilith would provide the opportunity for Zaid to betray his father and then become one of Ari's staunchest allies.

Lilith called Set to her as she stood on the bank of the river. Her son appeared next to her concerned about why his mother would call him to her. Lilith rarely called Set away from his post in Egypt.

"Mother?"

"I must ask a favor of you. You must travel to the palace of Ashurhassan and obscure yourself from their view. I need information about his sons," Lilith said as calmly as she was able.

"His sons?"

"When I recovered in the Underworld, Ashurhassan wooed Shiamat and together they bore two sons whom she named Lugal and Zaid. I believe Enlil is behind this. He will stop at nothing to see me suffer," Lilith whispered to her son.

Set's eyes glowed an ominous color of red and his pupils turned to those of the snake wrapped around his arm as the anger within him began to well at Enlil's continuous abuse of his Mother.

"If it is the last act I perform as a God, I shall make him suffer a thousand fold for what he has done to you!" The anger within Set seethed between each word as he spoke with Lilith.

"This is not your war to fight Set. I alone must take Enlil from his throne upon the heavens above us. He is a true Immortal the same as I. Though you are my child and are strong and beautiful, he could kill you if it was his desire. You must swear to me your most solemn word that you will not confront Enlil. I cannot bear the thought of losing you," Lilith thought as she touched Set's face and a single tear rolled down her cheek.

"I will obey your wishes, but only because I cannot stand to see you cry. Were it my choice, I would tear him from the Heavens and eat his heart!"

Set spread his massive wings and took flight. Lilith sat by the edge of the river and dangled her feet in the cool water as she waited for her son to return. Lilith waited next to the Euphrates for two days before Set appeared next to her. He gracefully landed behind her and his expression was one of displeasure.

"It is not at all as we had thought Mother. Zaid and Lugal are not Half Bloods. They are Pure Bloods, or at least as close to being a Pure Blood as they can be. I am not sure how it is possible, but King Ashurhassan is a Blood God. How could this be when he was not given your host?" Set asked her as he crossed his arms and looked down at his mother.

Lilith screamed out and the ground beneath them began to shake violently. Her anger caused all the living creatures within the river to die and the river to run red with blood.

"He has given Ashurhassan part of his host," Lilith hissed as her eyes turned black.

"That is not all Mother. He has a woman prisoner within the walls of his palace whose eyes are as blue as the ocean and hair that is as golden as the sun. She too is a Blood God. He holds her with the same intention that he has for Ari. He will use her as a breeder to create a race in his image, but we have an advantage to which he is not privy," Set said and then smiled deviously at Lilith.

"And what is this advantage?" Lilith asked with desire in her voice.

"He has charged his sons with guarding her so that she may not escape his hold on her, but he is unaware that Zaid loves her. Were you to plant the seed within him, he would love her in the darkness of the night and conceive a child with her. Zaid's betrayal of his father would cause them to flee his father's palace and seek solitude with Ari," Set's eyes began to shift colors as he spoke about his plan.

"You have done well my son to discover this. This will give us the advantage we need and set the prophecy into motion. Enlil did not plan on us discovering his deception. Go to Ensu and tell her what you have learned. I shall go to Zaid and implant the seeds of our deception."

Lilith disappeared and Set went to Ensu to tell her what he had learned about Ashurhassan's and Shiamat's sons. Lilith appeared inside Ashurhassan's palace, disguising herself with a glamour so as to hide her identity. She stood in the shadows and watched Zaid speak with the golden haired woman who was overwhelmed with grief. All she desired was to return to her homeland and her own people. The woman with whom Zaid spoke was a Blood God. Lilith thought to herself about the implication of her discovery. Only Enlil could have done this. None of the other Gods would go against her in this manner.

Lilith waited as the sun began to set and the colors of the evening sky appeared on the horizon. She watched as Zaid continued to attempt to comfort the overwrought beauty whom he called Amira. Lilith made herself like the wind and swirled around Zaid as she whispered to him in the dark corridor.

"Go to her this night and hold her within your arms. Love her and comfort her with your touch. She loves you and desires to be your wife, not his. Would you let him take her from you just as he has the others whom you have desired? Take what is rightfully yours and the pleasure you will share will be immeasurable," Lilith whispered as she swirled around Zaid.

Lilith stood in the entrance to Amira's room and watched as Zaid passed her. His love for her was very deep and genuine. There was no other woman he desired more than the lovely beauty who wept silently upon her bed as she tried to hide her tears from him. Zaid sat upon the edge of her bed and brushed her hair away from her face as she cried.

"I am sorry you long so deeply for your homeland. Can I do nothing to ease your sorrow? My land is not the same as yours, but there is beauty here if you desire to see it. Were it in my power, I would take you to your home on the gilded ship which brought you to me even though it would cause me great sadness," Zaid whispered as he tenderly touched Amira.

Lilith's words had been heard. She needed to watch them no longer and returned to the Temple at Eridu. Ensu and Shiamat were busily preparing the Great Hall for the arrival of several foreign emissaries who were bringing gifts to honor Lilith. Set sat patiently in the corner awaiting his mother's return. Set immediately stood before Lilith even appeared when he sensed her presence.

It saddened Lilith as she looked at Shiamat and how much she had aged. Shiamat had never asked Lilith to give her the gift of being a Blood Born. It saddened Lilith that one day her loyal friend would wither and die just as all the humans did. To Lilith, Shiamat embodied everything the humans were once designed to be and held within her the most desirable traits of all humanity. Shiamat was loyal, honest, and caring. There was no malice or hatred within Shiamat, only love lived within her frail human shell.

"Lilith," Shiamat said with glee as she looked up to Lilith standing behind Ensu.

"Liadan went to see to see Hammurabi again this morning. The city of Capurnicus thrives in Sephre's care and Hammurabi does what he can to keep them hidden," Shiamat said.

Lilith looked at Shiamat with curiosity when she spoke Ensu's true name.

"All is well Lilith. I have told them the truth. Ari and the others now know the truth behind who I am and about Ari's brother Quinn. I no longer have to hide behind a name which is not my own," Liadan said and smiled at Shiamat.

Shiamat had been like a mother to Liadan, just the same as Lilith had, but it had saddened Liadan to have to live behind a lie. Liadan knew that she must do this to protect her daughter and her son, but it did not make the pain any less difficult.

"Those who offered themselves into Ashurhassan's service will arrive here soon. He collects those who would willingly give their lives to him to become part of Ari's legion," Liadan said with little emotion.

"Your son will be among them Shiamat. You will finally be reunited with Zaid and his lovely wife Amira," Lilith whispered.

Shiamat swooned and fainted upon hearing Lilith's revelation. Set rushed across the room and caught Shiamat before she touched the floor. He carried Shiamat to her room and gently laid her upon the bed. Lilith sent Set to fetch some cold water, and Lilith gently wiped her face until Shiamat finally opened her eyes.

"I did not mean to cause you pain Shiamat. Please forgive me," Lilith whispered.

"I have not laid eyes upon my son in nearly ten years. Tell me, has he grown strong in my absence? Is he…" Shiamat stopped in mid-sentence. She did wish to hurt Lilith's feelings.

"He is like me Shiamat. I am sorry to be the one who must tell you. Both Zaid and Lugal are nearly Pure Bloods created in Ashurhassan's and Enlil's image. Enlil is in league with Ashurhassan against me. This was his way of using your children in an attempt to gain advantage. He will not succeed. Enlil placed within Ashurhassan a piece of his host after he became a Blood Born. I am sorry that I did not know Ashurhassan was the man who had fathered your sons. I had no way of knowing he would alter the blood of your children to make them pure. I should have protected you Shiamat. I should have kept you from harm, but I had no way of knowing that Enlil would do this."

Shiamat held Lilith's hand. She did not want her beloved friend to feel remorse for a matter which she had no control over. It was her choice and her choice alone to lay with Ashurhassan and conceive her children.

"Is he beautiful?" Shiamat asked.

"He is very pleasing to the eyes. You should take pride in your son. He is kind and loving the same as you. He does not mirror the image of his father in the least. I am sure he will be overjoyed at the thought of being reunited with his mother."

"Come, it will not be long before they will begin their journey to seek out Ari. His wife is as lovely as the stars in the Heavens and her eyes are just as blue. She carries Zaid's child within her. You will soon be the adored grandmother of a very unique child," Lilith said with pride.

The world of vampires was about to surround them in numbers greater than Lilith could have ever imagined, and her most perfect creation would be the one who would become their Queen.

Chapter Ten
Lover's Quarrel

The next several months passed quickly as Lilith stood in the shadows and watched Ari and Drake from afar. She took great satisfaction in watching Liadan's child and how quickly Ari had taken to her role as Queen. Ari put the welfare of others above her, and she viewed the humans as frail and weak the same as Lilith. To Ari, the humans were nothing more than pawns she could move and control at her will.

At last, Lilith had another who understood the place of the humans within the world of vampires. Now Lilith would be able to exact her revenge against Enlil. He had meddled in her affairs long enough, and she had not yet forgiven him for crucifying her on the Tree of Woe. She would make him pay with what he held most dear, his precious humans.

Enlil fought Lilith at every turn and used his prior knowledge about her to his advantage. When Zaid and Amira arrived at the Ziggurat at Eridu to seek sanctuary with Ari, Lilith disguised herself and listened to their thoughts as they waited in the corridor. Once Lilith was able to lay her eyes upon Zaid, she knew the truth. Enlil had given a piece of his host to Ashurhassan after Lilith had been invoked during Ashurhassan's Blood Ceremony. When Shiamat gave birth to Lugal, and then to his younger brother Zaid, Enlil had given them blood from the Bowl of Velspruga. Zaid and Lugal were as close to a Pure Blood as a vampire could become without having been born from the union of two Blood Gods.

Enlil carefully planned each step he took. He sought ways to be able to fool and misguide Lilith in her quest.

Lilith was no fool and she knew exactly what Enlil was planning. Lilith called to Enuki to lay a trap for Enlil. One that would keep him occupied while Lilith laid her well thought plan into place.

"Enuki, call Ningirama and the three of us will raise the storms and flood the beloved lands of his humans. I wish to see the rivers run red with blood and all life within them perish," Lilith whispered as she leaned over Enuki.

"And what does Lilith of Sumeria hope to gain from this," Enuki asked.

"When have you ever been one to turn away from doing what you do best Enuki?" Lilith asked. She was coy in the manner in which she spoke with Enuki. Lilith knew he could not refuse her when she asked him to embrace his true nature.

"What shall I receive in return?" Enuki asked as he circled Lilith.

Lilith drew a deep breath and the wind circled her; causing the black gown she was wearing to ripple softly like reflections on a pool of water. She could use the sensual part of her nature to convince Enuki to do whatever she desired.

"Do you desire a woman to stand at your side Enuki, for if that is your wish, then I shall have my son create one for you," Lilith whispered. Her breath was sweet and enticing as she spoke to Enuki, and he eagerly agreed.

Lilith disappeared and appeared in the temple of her son Set. Astarte laid across his lap wrapped in white linen with strands of gold woven into her hair. It pleased Lilith to see how much her son had grown to love the woman who was once only a conquest to him. Lilith waited patiently as Set leaned over Astarte as she held him and kissed her.

Astarte blushed when she realized Lilith was watching them. She stood and bowed to Lilith as Lilith walked past her toward her son. She paused briefly and laid her hand on Astarte's shoulder.

"Do not bow to me sweet child for you are now a Goddess in your own right."

Set stood and stretched his massive black wings behind him, then lowered them behind his back as he embraced his Mother.

"Mother, it has been much too long since my eyes last saw you," Set said as he took Lilith's hand and led her to the chair next to his.

"I am sorry I have been gone from you for so long Set. It was never my intention. Enlil has attempted to out step my every move. I must keep him occupied while Ari grows stronger. Once she has embraced her darkness completely, even Enlil will not be able to touch her." Lilith's eyes turned red as she paused. "I have struck a bargain with the other Gods, and they will aid me. I have one last condition to fulfill before I will see my desires granted."

"And what is the one last condition they require of you?" Set asked.

"I must provide Enuki with an Immortal bride."

"And you desire for me to create her?" Set asked his mother as he reclined in his chair.

"Yes, it would be my request of you. I do not want to give Enuki too perfect an Immortal woman. If I create her through sacred rites, she would mirror me too closely. Enuki must have a woman who is like him, one who jovial and quick to forgive his trickster ways. If she is born of me, she will possess a small amount of darkness and may grow tired of his antics. Whereas, if it were you who embraced her, she would retain more of her human nature and be more inclined toward forgiveness."

Set contemplated his Mother's words and motioned for one of his Priests. Set's Priest stood before him as Set told him which Priestess should be brought before him. The Priest left immediately to locate the young woman.

The Priest returned with the young Priestess who immediately laid her head at Set's feet. Set motioned for the Priest to leave as he leaned forward and touched the young woman's hair. He looked up at Astarte who stood glaring at him with her arms crossed.

"Leave us," Set screamed.

Astarte spun around and left only a trail of mist in her wake. Set slid his hand under the young girl's chin and tilted her head back so he could see her face.

"Will she do, Mother?" Set asked.

Lilith nodded her head as she reclined against the back of her chair and watched her son with pride. Set laid the woman down on the divan and slowly untied the braided strands of fabric that fastened her dress. He slid her dress down over her shoulders exposing her round and ample breasts. As Set kissed the young Priestess, Lilith watched all the girl's inhibitions melt at her son's touch.

Set knelt between the young woman's legs as he placed his hand on her shoulder to hold her down beneath him as he sank his teeth into the flesh of her breast. Set forced his blood into the screaming Priestess as he slid his leg over hers to help hold her down as she struggled against him. Lilith watched silently as the young girl fought to push Set away from her as his blood coursed through her frail human body. The Priestess began to resist him less and Set leaned away from her as he pierced his wrist with his fangs.

Set placed his hand behind her neck and held his wrist above her as he allowed his blood to drip into her mouth. He gently laid her down and buried his teeth in the flesh of her neck as he took her blood. When he released the poor woman, she was already beginning to bruise where he had bitten her. Lilith stood and covered the Priestess with the cotton blanket that was draped over the back of the divan. Together Set and Lilith waited for the moment when she would awaken as a vampire.

"Astarte is most jealous of your actions my son. You should take care not to bruise her feelings that way," Lilith said as she raised her eyes to look at her son.

Set walked into the center of the temple and spread his wings out so they could catch the rays of the sun which streamed through the glass atrium above him.

"She will forgive me this one pleasure I have, in time," Set said as he folded his shimmering black wings behind him.

"Do you allow her the same indulgence?" Lilith asked sternly.

Set laughed at his Mother's suggestion and his lack of regard for Astarte's feelings angered her greatly. She appeared in front of Set and struck him sharply across his cheek.

"Have you learned nothing in the years you have watched me suffer in silence?" Lilith asked.

Lilith was overcome with guilt for striking her beloved child. Lilith placed her hands on either side of Set's face as she spoke to him.

"Though women are strong, they are frail. One day if you hurt her too deeply, she will lose the ability to love you. Is that what you wish?"

Set turned his eyes away from Lilith and stared at the temple floor. His conceit about his power over the young mortal Priestess had led him to act in a manner which he knew had hurt Astarte.

"I will speak to her. Stay here and watch over the young girl. I will return as soon as I have calmed her anger," Lilith whispered.

Lilith appeared in Astarte's temple and watched Astarte's Priests flee from her. The inside of the temple was in shambles and only a few items were left unbroken in the wake of her anger.

"You must quell your anger toward him Astarte. Men know not the feelings of a woman's heart. It is hard for them to understand us completely," Lilith said as Astarte continued to smash various statues within her grasp. Lilith laughed loudly at Astarte's show of anger in her presence.

"I find very little amusing about his behavior," Astarte yelled.

"I do not condone his behavior with my laughter dear one. I was only enjoying how vigorously you have chosen to embrace your title of Warrior Goddess," Lilith said and smiled.

Astarte fell to her knees as she tried to conceal her tears. Lilith knelt next her, and Astarte laid her head on Lilith's shoulder.

"Why must he take them before me in that manner? How would he feel if I did the same?" Astarte asked.

"Men do not always think with their hearts. But I know it in my heart to be true that there is no other he desires more than he desires you. I have known this since the first time I saw him with you many years ago. You bring to light the best in my son. Can you not find it in your heart to forgive him once more?"

Astarte could not argue with Lilith's words. There was no other she longed for the way she desired Set. His touch set her body on fire, and his mere presence aroused her. She knew she could not stay angry with him even though she desired to punish Set for his insensitive behavior.

"He will not ever behave that way again in your presence. I have already cautioned him about the error of his ways where you are concerned. I am sure he will lavish you with many gifts in the days to come to win back your favor," Lilith whispered.

"You defended me?" Astarte asked. "But Set is your son."

"Yes, he is my creation but you are a woman and deserve to be treated with kindness and respect. I know all too well how dark a woman's heart can become when she is hurt by the man she loves. He will never do that again, this I can promise you."

Lilith helped Astarte to stand as her Priests peered into the room as they tried to discern if it was safe for them to return. Lilith beckoned the Priests to return and begin cleaning the rubble left in Astarte's anger. Lilith brushed Astarte's long locks behind her ear and kissed her on the forehead before she returned to Set.

Set paced in front of the Priestess who was now beginning to stir. He appeared frantic in his behavior as though he were afraid Astarte would not forgive him.

"She will forgive you in time, however, I must caution you. Your actions have hurt her very deeply Set. A mere apology like those of the past will not be enough for her to forgive you this time."

Lilith approached the divan and watched the young woman as she moaned in her sleep. It would not be long before she would awaken and take her place as one of Lilith's many children. She knew Enuki would be pleased with her offering. Her deception against Enlil could soon begin. Lilith took the young woman into her arms and appeared before Enuki.

The first one from whom she fed would be the one the young Priestess would be bonded to for the rest of her immortal life. Lilith held her hand as the Priestess took her first taste of blood from Enuki. Her eyes were a soft shade of blue that reminded Lilith of the sea. Enuki could not have been more pleased.

"How is it then you desire to trick Enlil?" Enuki asked as he cradled his new love in his arms.

"I wish to create havoc upon the land and thus endanger his beloved humans. He will be so occupied in his attempts to save them, Enlil will forget his desire for revenge where I am concerned, and I can care for the children of my own creation," Lilith whispered.

"Ningirama has unleashed the rivers and flooded the lands west of Ur and Eridu. It is whispered Enlil already seeks his consul to discover why he would do this. I am sure Ningirama will tell him he is angry with the humans for the lack of respect they show to him," Enuki said.

"Good. This shall give me the opportunity I need. While I spread devastation across the world of his beloved mortals, he will forget about my children," Lilith said as she touched the Priestess Enuki still held in his arms. "What is your name child?"

"Asrahaia," the Priestess whispered.

"Be kind to Asrahaia, Enuki, and love her gently," Lilith whispered as she faded from their view.

Lilith was not only a Mother Goddess but was also desolation in its purest form. She unleashed great swells upon seas. She called forth the fire from the sleeping mountains and caused the ground to quake beneath the feet of the terrified mortals. Great plagues unleashed themselves in droves against the humans as Lilith took pleasure in destroying the land of Enlil's treasured and prized creatures. She embraced her anger and released it into the world of man. So great was the pleasure she took from the devastation she had unleashed, Lilith could not feel the tragedy that was about to befall her.

Liadan appeared beside Lilith as she called the gale force winds and sank the sailing vessels on the Armenian Sea. When Lilith turned to face Liadan, she saw her heart was filled with sadness. Lilith immediately feared Liadan's appearance had to do with Ari.

"Mother," Liadan whispered. "Shiamat has fallen ill."

In her rage and her anger, Lilith had forgotten how much time had passed. It had been nearly thirty years since she had been home. Liadan wrapped her arms around Lilith as they vanished and appeared in the temple at Eridu.

Shiamat's breathing was labored and erratic as she slept. Lilith sat on the edge of Shiamat's bed and pulled her covers around her.

"How long has she been this ill?" Lilith asked.

"Nearly three days. I would have come for you, but she seemed to be so much better until this morning," Liadan whispered.

"Where is Zaid?"

"He is at the compound in Egypt with Sephre. Do you wish for me to send for him?" Liadan asked.

Lilith was torn by what she should do next. If she called Zaid to her so he may speak to his mother before she left this world, it could endanger the whereabouts of Ari and the others. Lilith knew Ari was still trapped in her dark slumber. She did not know if Ari would be vulnerable to an attack if Enlil discovered her. It was a decision Lilith did not wish to make.

"No," Lilith whispered as she laid down next to Shiamat.

"As you wish," Liadan said and went to the door to allow Lilith her final moments alone with Shiamat.

"Can the Priests do nothing for her?" Lilith asked.

"It is only a matter of time they said. She has the withering sickness. There is nothing they can do."

Liadan left Lilith alone with Shiamat. Lilith watched her as she slept and grew tormented by the pending death of her beloved friend. Lilith held her hand into the dark of night as she prayed for Shiamat to regain consciousness. As the sun began to break, Shiamat opened her eyes. Lilith's eyes filled with tears.

"Why did you not allow me to grant you the gift of immortality? I do not wish for you to leave me," Lilith said softly.

"I have lived a beautiful life. Do not shed tears for me Lilith. Each moment I served, you gave me joy, and I would not trade any memories I have, be they good or bad, for one minute of immortality. I was not meant to be like you. I will meet you again one day. I have only one request that I would ask of you." Shiamat's voice became strained, and it was difficult for Lilith to understand her.

"I will do whatever you ask," Lilith said as she squeezed Shiamat's hand.

"I would like for Nergal to carry me to the Underworld and grant me safe passage. I would want no other to care for me than the one who loves you."

They were the last words Shiamat would say. Lilith held Shiamat in her arms as she died and her grief was so great she cried tears of blood. Lilith cried for several hours before she was able to call Nergal to her. She could not speak as Nergal lifted Shiamat's lifeless body from her arms. The only human that Lilith had ever held in the same high regard as she did her vampire children was now gone.

Nergal disappeared with Shiamat and carried her through the sixteen gates which led to his world before he returned for Lilith. Lilith did not fight Nergal as he took her into his arms. She wept uncontrollably as she laid her head against his chest. If Lilith had been able to bear a child, she would have wanted that child to be Shiamat.

Lilith was immersed in her grief so deeply she did not speak for several months. She refused to take any form of nourishment whether it was food or Nergal's blood. Lilith grew frail in appearance as she allowed her grief and torment over Shiamat's death to become her only focus. Nergal grew more and more concerned as each day passed. He knew he could not seek the help or council of the other Gods for fear of them discovering Ari's location. He could not stand by and watch Lilith wither away. His love for her was too great.

Nergal carried her meal to their bed and placed it on the bed next to her just has he had done for the last two moons. Again, Lilith pushed the food away from her just as she did each day when Nergal came to her. Nergal took the tray and tossed it across the room where it slammed loudly into the wall of the crystal cave.

"I will not stand idly by as you punish yourself for her death," Nergal said as he grabbed Lilith forcefully by her arm.

Nergal drew his dagger and plunged it into the flesh of his shoulder. His blood ran across his chest and dripped onto the bed as he held Lilith down beneath him.

"You will take my blood Lilith, even if I must force you to do so," Nergal said angrily as he continued to hold Lilith down.

Though his voice was filled with anger, Lilith could hear the worry in his words as he yelled at her. Nergal was apprehensive about restraining her this way given what had happened to Lilith in the past, but he felt it was the only way he could bring her back to him.

"You cannot continue this way," Nergal whispered as he released Lilith.

Nergal slid his hand into Lilith's hair and pulled her toward him. His blood smelled sweet. Lilith became filled with lust as she took his blood. Her eyes returned to their beautiful lavender color that Nergal adored.

"Love me and make forget," Lilith whispered.

Nergal held Lilith in his arms as she cried, but he would not make love to her. Nergal would not allow Lilith to succumb to her desire in her grief. He could not take advantage of her that way even though it was what Lilith desired. His love for her was too great, so Nergal simply held Lilith until she fell asleep.

Lilith stayed with Nergal for many years and her sadness never lessened until the day Nergal surrendered to Lilith's wishes and loved her. As she lay across his chest, she was finally able to remember her Shiamat without sadness or tears.

"I have never felt sadness like this before. Is this how death affects the mortals?" Lilith asked Nergal.

"For some, yes."

"I have embraced my anger, however I could not do so with my sadness. I do not believe I wish to ever feel sadness again," Lilith whispered as she moved her head onto Nergal's shoulder.

"It is a tender side of you that I did not know. Though I did not wish for you to become so enveloped in your grief, I am honored it was with me that you chose to share your despair. I love you Lilith. It was all I could do to watch your heart grieve so deeply. My only wish is that you will never have to feel that pain again."

It was the first time Lilith had ever heard the words I love you spoken to her. It caused her to weep as she lay across Nergal's chest.

"Please no more tears," Nergal whispered as he held her tightly.

Nergal sensed this time Lilith's tears were somehow different as he held her. For the first time in Lilith's life, she was able to cry tears of joy.

Chapter Eleven
The Catacombs of the Firenzeans

Lilith remained with Nergal for many years before she decided to return to the world of the mortals. She knew it would be difficult for her to leave Nergal's crystal cave within the Underworld. She had grown to love him in a manner she did not believe was possible. Lilith missed her vampire children and longed to be close to them.

Lilith sat on the end of their bed with her head down as she waited for Nergal to return. She did not know how she was going to tell Nergal that she must leave him once more.

Nergal knew Lilith was going to leave before she told him. He could feel the longing in her heart. She had been away from those she regarded as her children for nearly nine hundred years. Ari was now the supreme regent of the vampire race. Lilith had not interceded when Ari and her family were threatened by Xerxes in Persia at Nergal's insistence. He had told her that if Ari were to prove herself as their Queen, she needed to do it on her own.

Nergal stood at the entrance to their bedchamber and watched Lilith as she sat on the end of their bed. She was so beautiful in his eyes. It saddened him that he had never been able to give her a child. Nergal knew that the deep sadness Lilith bore was her desire to have a child. He also knew that it was An who had taken this grace away from her without her knowledge. It was her judgment for orchestrating the death of Lahar at the hands of Ashnan.

Lilith slowly raised her eyes to meet his when she felt Nergal's presence in the room. She did not wish to tell him she was leaving. She wondered if it would have been better if she had just left without telling him.

"I will wait for you my love," Nergal whispered as he sat next to her.

"It is not fair for me to expect you to wait for my return. What if I should be gone for another two thousand years? No man should live that long without love." Lilith whispered.

"How many years did you exist without knowing the bliss of love Lilith? How many years was it before you could find it within your heart to allow yourself to love me? Why do you believe I never took another wife after Set killed Ereskigal? There is only room in my heart for one woman Lilith, and that is you."

His words made it even more difficult for her leave him. Lilith leaned against Nergal as he sat quietly next to her. She knew if she asked him to come with her Nergal would decline. As long as the humans had need for him to carry them to the next world, Nergal would not abandon his crystalline cave.

"I will be here waiting for you when you decide to return home," Nergal whispered and then kissed her.

Lilith could see the tears in his eyes as he turned away from her. Lilith stood before him and leaned down to whisper in his ear. She placed Nergal's hand on her chest.

"I will keep your love here, and it shall keep me whole."

Lilith disappeared and left Nergal alone as he hung his head and rested it in his hands. He knew it would be several millennia before he could love her again.

Lilith appeared in Southern Velch. Though Velch was a small city in comparison to the others which dotted the countryside of Etruria, it bustled just the same. The scent of the market with its fresh fruits, dried meats, and perfumeries was a delicacy to her senses. Lilith had not stood in the center of a bustling marketplace since she had resided in the temple at Eridu.

Lilith admired the jewelry the women wore and the strange style of their dress. As she wandered along the stone streets, several Firenzeans followed her. Lilith could hear them whispering behind her and smiled. Her children had recognized her. She swept her long black hair over her shoulder as she leaned forward to smell the perfumes and scented oils on the table in front of her. Lilith had no currency with which to purchase the woman's wares, which she soon found was not an issue. Each item Lilith had touched was quickly picked up and paid for by the four vampires who followed her. Lilith stopped and turned around. They quickly disappeared into one of the many small alleys.

Lilith closed her eyes and called them to her.

"There is no need to hide from me my children. Come, I will not hurt you," Lilith thought.

She stood in the shadow cast by one of the tents as they stepped out of their hiding places. Lilith's eyes glowed a darker shade of lavender than usual as she gazed at her children. Her hair blew softly around her face as the wind danced around her. Lilith could feel the joy in the hearts of the vampires who surrounded her as they touched her. They were like children in so many ways still with the innocent curiosity they possessed toward her. Their touch lessened the sadness Lilith felt at having to leave her beloved Nergal. Lilith could find happiness until she could return to him by being surrounded by her beautiful vampire children.

"I am Cassea. Please, accompany us to our home," the young girl whispered as she touched Lilith's arm and then quickly pulled her hand away.

Lilith took Cassea's hand in hers and followed her through the narrow streets of Velch to a large bath house. Cassea removed the torch by the door and motioned for Lilith to follow her inside. Cassea looked over her shoulder to ensure the sentry was still standing in the doorway as she pushed on the wall to open the secret entrance to the catacombs. Lilith followed behind Cassea as she stepped into the narrow passageway as the hidden door closed behind them.

The catacombs where illuminated with the light from hundreds of oil lamps and candles that hung from iron fasteners in the stone walls. Cassea extinguished the torch in a bucket of water and waited for the next door to be opened by the second sentry.

Lilith was in awe of the city that was revealed when the sentry opened the door. There was little difference between the city she now stood in compared to the one which was above her. Cassea took Lilith through the center of the market to her home. She paused at the humble wooden door that led to her home before she opened it.

"Had we known we would be graced by your presence, we would have had much better accommodations waiting for you. My home is very humble compared to what you are accustomed to I am sure," Cassea said and then opened the door to her home.

Lilith stepped inside and waited for Cassea. Lilith noticed the floors where covered in the finest Persian rugs and many of the statues which adorned her home where carved from solid malachite or lapis. Two large rolled back divans sat across from each other in front of a small fireplace. The walls were painted a rich color of burnt red and accented by brilliantly painted murals which depicted everyday life in Velch. Lilith thought Cassea's home was very beautiful.

"The others will be along as soon as it is safe. They will bring everything with them that you will need. I will give you my room until we can find you your own private quarters," Cassea said as she lowered her eyes in reverence and parted the fabric which hung over the entrance to her bedroom.

"You are most generous and kind Cassea," Lilith whispered as she stepped into Cassea's room.

Lilith had not considered that they would recognize her so easily. If she were to stay in Velch she would need to create a glamour to disguise herself. Though the vampires of Velch would still be able to recognize her, a glamour would allow her to walk among the humans without drawing their gaze. The warm olive color of the Firenzeans skin was dark in comparison to Lilith's soft milky white complexion. Lilith stood in front of the Venetian mirror that hung in Cassea's room and slid her fingers through her hair. As she did, her luminous, shiny black hair became a sultry shade of deep brown with gold and red highlights.

Lilith admired herself in the mirror as her skin came to match the warm olive color of Cassea's. Now Lilith mirrored every other citizen of Velch. She could not be sure that Enlil would not search for her now that he knew she was no longer with Nergal in the Underworld. Though he would recognize her scent immediately if he were near her, at least his many minions would not be able to recognize her by sight alone.

Cassea returned with the three other vampires who had followed Lilith through the market. Their arms were filled with flowing gowns, jewelry, and other fine womanly trappings. Cassea motioned for them to lay the articles on the bed as Lilith smiled at their thoughtfulness.

"We would be honored if you would preside over the blood feast tonight," the young man whispered as he knelt at Lilith's feet.

Lilith tilted her head as she looked at him. He was so young and newly born as a vampire. She could feel the racing of his blood and the stillness of his heart. The young man who knelt before her was not a Blood Born. He was a Hybrid. Lilith slid her fingers through his long curly dark black hair.

"What is your name child?" Lilith asked him.

"I am Petronius of the Firenzean Clan, once the son of Verbius," the young man said softly as he trembled at her touch.

Lilith wondered if they all would tremble in her presence the way Petronius did or if it was merely how newly born he was.

"Tell me, what is this blood feast you speak of," Lilith said as she sat in the chair in the corner of Cassea's room.

"Once each week the humans provide us with those who would willing give us their blood to sustain us in exchange for our protection. The Roman's have come to Firenzea and Velch on many occasions to attempt to overthrow the Senators that reside here. We have no use for the Romans or their ways. They are brutal and cruel. The ways of the citizens of Velch are peaceful, and they desire to keep it this way. The first time the Roman's came to our city, they took many of the women by force. We could not stand idly by and watch them hurt the members of our human families that still remained, so we interceded on behalf of the humans. It is an arrangement that serves us both well," Cassea said.

"I have decided to reside in Velch for a period of time. The four of you must never call me by my true name. It could endanger you and bring a vengeful wrath down upon you. As long I chose to live among you, you will refer to me as Aranthe," Lilith said sternly. "The four of you shall be my personal attendants. Now we must plan the story of my arrival so that my identity shall remain hidden."

The four of them talked well into the night until it was only an hour before the blood feast was due to begin. They conceived a story about Aranthe, how she had come to Velch to hide amongst the Firenzean Clan. They would tell the story of how she was the daughter of a quite well known Senator named Romulus from Rome. Aranthe, in a moment of passion, was embraced by a senior Roman vampire. Aranthe had then fled Rome to escape execution by her father for her indiscretions, lack of humility, and her inability to keep her virginity intact prior to her marriage. They would tell the citizens of Velch that Aranthe's infidelity would be viewed as an act against her father.

Lilith prepared for the evening that lied before her. She eagerly anticipated attending the blood feast. It would mark the first time in her life that Lilith would be completely surrounded by her creations. Lilith stood before the Venetian mirror and combed her hair as Petronius selected a gown from the many he had brought her. He chose a deep purple gown that complemented the soft lavender shade of her eyes along with several pieces of jewelry to accent her dress. Petronius knelt at Lilith's feet as he whispered to her.

"For your approval Aranthe."

Petronius spoke so softly as he knelt before her it would have been difficult for a mere mortal to hear him. Lilith stroked his long curls and smiled down at him.

"You do not have to whisper in my presence child. How long has it been since your old life ceased and your new one began?" Lilith asked.

She knew he could not have been a vampire for more than a year at the most. He was still nervous in the presence of others, and it was easy for Lilith to see that Cassea kept another in his presence at all times. It was difficult for Petronius to be near the humans and the way they smelled. His blood raced continuously. Petronius had not yet learned to quell the racing of the bloodlust.

Petronius could not answer her. He trembled as he knelt before her. Lilith gently lifted his face toward her so she could see his brilliant blue eyes, the eyes of a Hybrid.

"Do not fear me," Lilith whispered as she touched his face.

Lilith's touch soothed Petronius and soon his blood began to slow to a more smooth and even pace. She looked at him with loving eyes as she continued to soothe him with her touch. He could not be more than twenty years old in human years. He was still a child in many ways.

"Come," Lilith whispered as she motioned for him to sit next to her. "Tell me about your life."

Petronius was still shaking as he sat next to her.

"My father, Verbius, was a good man. He was taken when the Romans first came to our city. His death was very brutal. They forced my mother to watch as he was whipped to death. The flesh was peeled from his back as they beat him before my mother. I watched through the grates beneath him as they killed my father. Though I wanted to fight the Romans, my mother hid me beneath the city so I would not be captured. It was not long after my father's death my mother took her own life. Cassea allowed me to dwell with her in Firenzea, our city beneath Velch. I lived with her for nearly five years before her creator embraced me. She protected me from the others as I was the only human who lived within the city of vampires."

"What is the name of Cassea's creator?" Lilith asked.

"His name is Lucius. He traveled here from Crete, or perhaps Minoa. No one really knows for sure where he came from and why he came to Velch," Petronius replied.

"I see. Has it been painful for you to live your new life away from those you once loved?"

Petronius did not answer Lilith, and he did not have to. The words were written in his blood.

"Does Lucius live among you?" Lilith asked.

"No. Lucius is cruel. He does not know about our city. He knows only about the blood feast. We allow him to attend only to keep the location of our city from him. The feast is held far from here. We should hasten your preparations for this night or we will be late," Petronius whispered.

Petronius took the silver comb from Lilith's hand and finished combing her hair. He pulled her now rich brown hair away from her face and secured it with two silver combs. Lilith placed the amethyst cabochon around her neck, and Petronius fastened it for her. As Lilith dressed before the young vampire, she knew in her heart that Lucius was somehow connected to Enlil. She just did not know how.

Lilith's lack of modesty as she dressed before Petronius caused him to blush and avert his eyes. She smiled at how demure he seemed in her presence. That would change soon enough. Lilith took pleasure in his company.

Lilith followed Cassea and Petronius through the catacombs, and they emerged in another part of Velch. Lilith was impressed at the measures they took to conceal their whereabouts from the rest of the world. Cassea opened a door that led into the rear of another home, and they stepped into the street as though they were leaving the home of an old friend.

As Lilith walked through the streets of Velch, the humans were intoxicated by her lovely scent. They nearly swooned as she passed them. The vampires which lined the stone path leading to the hall bowed to her as she walked the remaining few steps to the hall entrance.

Lilith entered the grand hall that nearly resembled temple ruins and was seated between Cassea and Petronius. When Lucius entered the room, Lilith felt a strange familiarity to him. She watched him closely as he took his place across from her at the table. Lilith parted her lips ever so slightly as Lucius stared at her.

"To whom do I owe the pleasure of thanking for seating me across from such a lovely beauty?" Lucius asked as he reached across the table taking Lilith's hand in his and then kissed her hand.

"This is Aranthe. She hails from Rome," Cassea said.

"A Roman vampire here in Velch? Have you come to discover our secrets?" Lucius said coyly as he continued to stare at Lilith.

"I am but a humble guest my lord," Lilith replied carefully.

Lilith watched as the Hybrids began to escort the humans into the center of the hall. It disturbed Lilith that majority of them were women.

"Have you no men who would offer themselves?" Lilith asked as she leaned in close to Cassea.

Cassea said nothing as she touched Lilith so she could see what she was thinking. She did not want Lucius to hear her thoughts. Cassea showed Lilith the true reason behind why all the human offerings were mostly women.

"Does it displease you to dine on the same sex? I thought Romans were more free-spirited than that," Lucius said and laughed loudly.

Before Lucius could finish laughing, Lilith was standing behind him with her hands on his shoulders. She leaned over him, and as she exhaled, Lucius was enveloped in the rapture of her touch.

"Careful young one, I am much older than you think," Lilith whispered in his ear as she drew her fingers across his shoulder and around the front of his neck. "It would not be wise to anger me."

All eyes in the room turned toward Lilith as she stood behind Lucius. Petronius stood immediately with his hand firmly clutching the hilt of his dagger. Cassea laid her hand on his forearm to signal him to withdraw his advance. Petronius took his place next to Cassea, but his eyes never left Lucius. Lilith appeared next to Petronius and sat next to him. She could sense the fear within Lucius. He had never encountered a vampire like her before; her touch had filled him with not only excitement but also dread.

"I apologize if I have offended you," Lucius said as he lowered his eyes.

Lilith did not respond to the apology Lucius offered to her. Instead, she watched as her many children began to circle the humans in the center of the hall. She watched eagerly as her children took the blood of the humans. The scent of their flowing blood and the lust she could feel within her beautiful creations filled Lilith with ecstasy as she watched them. It had been many years since Lilith had embraced this type of euphoria. She knew she could not embrace and nor feed from any of those who came to offer themselves this night. As soon as her teeth pierced their flesh, they would be filled with pleasure followed by death. Lilith understood it was too risky an undertaking and could lead to her discovery.

Petronius led one of the few male humans to Lilith's side. He withdrew his dagger and slit the man's throat as he knelt before Lilith. Cassea took one of the chalices from the table as did Petronius to catch the man's blood as it flowed from the gaping wound. They placed the chalices before Lilith and were careful not to bow to her as they did so.

Lilith watched Lucius' expression over what he had just witnessed as she placed the first chalice to her lips. Blood trickled down the side of her cheek as she drank which only fed the desire now growing in Lucius to possess Aranthe.

Lilith placed the chalice on the table in front of her before she spoke.

"I know what your heart desires Lucius. I must warn you now. You will never possess me. My heart belongs to another and there my loyalty shall lie till the end of my days," Lilith whispered as her eyes became blood red.

Lucius smiled at Lilith wickedly. He took pleasure in her answer to him. She would be a worthy conquest in his eyes.

"You take not their lives on your own but instead allow another to do so for you. May I ask why?" Lucius asked.

"That is a difficult question for me to answer in a manner in which you would be able to understand," Lilith whispered as she leaned across the table before taking the other chalice in her hand.

Her words infuriated Lucius. Never had a woman been so bold, brazen, and so rude to him before in his life. Were it not for all the vampires who surrounded him, Lucius would have attacked Lilith.

Lilith ignored Lucius as she turned her attention toward her children as she watched them drain the blood of the humans within the hall. Her vengeance against Enlil was nearing full circle. Her vampires would lay waste to all of mankind.

Chapter Twelve
The Second War Rages

Lilith grew content as she was surrounded by her children amongst the Firenzean Clan. Petronius matured into a vampire who exhibited an immense amount of self-control with her guidance. He learned to quell the racing of his blood and the pain of the bloodlust. Lilith was pleased when Cassea took Petronius as her husband and bonded with him. She had grown very fond of them in the many years she had lived with them. Though Lilith attempted to control her thoughts about Liadan, and how much she missed her, it was difficult for her to do so. She longed to see the one woman she regarded as her daughter and to speak to her about Ari. But Lilith knew she could endanger Ari if Enlil discovered Liadan had come to visit Lilith, so Lilith continued to be happy living amongst her many children until Enlil discovered her whereabouts.

As Lilith walked early one morning to the port to watch the sunrise over the sea, her thoughts wandered aimlessly till she came to the pier. As she dangled her feet in the warm waters of the sea, she thought about her once lovely home in Sumer. She missed the dry air and fresh smell of the Euphrates River. Most of all, Lilith missed Nergal. Lilith's longing and sorrow was so great it caused the skies above her to open and rain began to fall. Enlil watched as the storms over his beloved Earth began to form. He had seen these same storms before. He knew exactly who had unwittingly caused them.

As Lilith watched the sun's golden rays dance across the morning sea, she felt the wind dance around her as it once had in her beloved home. This wind was different and she knew all too well who controlled this wind. As

Lilith glanced over her shoulder, she saw Enlil appear behind her. He leaned down over Lilith and laid his hands upon her shoulders. Lilith stiffened at his touch and pulled away from Enlil.

"Have you grown shy in my absence Lilith?" Enlil whispered.

"Do not touch me Enlil. My heart no longer belongs to you. I would have thought you would have realized this many years ago."

"Yes, I know. It is now my son whom you allow to ravish you as I once did," Enlil said coldly.

Lilith vanished and appeared behind Enlil. Her eyes turned black as the anger she had once believed she had been able to let go began to return.

"Do not speak about your son that way. He is kind and loving toward me. Those are two traits your black heart will never possess or be able to fully understand," Lilith screamed.

She struck Enlil and the force behind her strength caught him off guard. Enlil stumbled which caused Lilith to laugh. Lilith could see the anger now raging within Enlil as he glared at her.

"You are still the spoiled son of a Supreme God. Little about you has changed over the centuries Enlil. Go home to your wife. Let me live my life in peace."

"I will kill all that you hold dear, Lilith. I will make your children suffer just as you have made mine," Enlil whispered as he touched her.

The longing she once had for Enlil still resided deep within Lilith and his touch startled her. She pushed Enlil away from her as the sky above her began to darken.

"Have you so conveniently forgotten Enlil or should I remind you? I am An and Ki's first born child. For years you attempted to hide this from me. Your jealousy will be your undoing. The Gods will stand against you just as they did before then it will be I who laughs when you fall from the heavens."

Enlil disappeared in a flash of light so bright that Lilith was forced to shield her eyes. Lilith called to Cassea and bade her to take all the vampires of Firenzea into hiding. The war was about to begin.

Lilith knew she could not win this war without the support of the other Gods. She called to Inanna, and she appeared before Lilith as she stood by the sea.

"This will end badly for all involved Lilith," Inanna said.

"I have many who would support me. His behavior has not changed. Surely the other Gods have tired of his juvenal behavior," Lilith replied.

"Many of the Gods have faded Lilith. They have become weak without the love of the humans who once worshipped them. Our days, I fear, are numbered. There will always be a belief in the one true God, and so long as there is, Enlil will always be powerful. I have been very fortunate. The love of the humans has carried my worship to many lands far from our beautiful Sumer. I live still because of this."

"What has happened to the Well of Velspruga?" Lilith asked her.

"Enlil has hidden it somewhere upon the Earth. We know not where he has placed it. Nergal lives and is strong since there must always be a counterpart, an opposite to what the humans believe in. Do not concern yourself with his safety."

Lilith pulled the hood of her cloak over her head and smiled at Inanna as her eyes glowed brilliant red.

"Where are you going Lilith?" Inanna asked.

"To the ones I know will help me. I go to call the Jhinn."

Lilith raised her eyes toward the Heavens and smiled. She knew that Enlil watched her silently from above. Lightning struck the ground surrounding Lilith before she disappeared.

The sand swirled around Lilith as she appeared in the desert outside of Sardis. The Jhinn were created many millennia ago in the first Immortal War. Those who fell upon the battlefield of the Gods who were re-animated by Enlil and became the Jhinn. Highly feared once they returned to Earth, the Jhinn came to despise Enlil for the curse he had placed upon them. Though the Jhinn were peaceful, the humans made war with them because they feared them so greatly. Lilith had to secretly admit their appearance was quite frightening yet immensely beautiful.

The Jhinn had royal blue eyes which glowed at all times. They spoke the language of the ancient Sumerian Gods so the humans could not understand them. The skin of the Jhinn appeared hard and wrinkled like layers of poorly tanned leather with an eerie blue cast to their skin. They carried staffs which they had crafted from the Tree of Woe that could drain the life from anyone they touched. They could call lightning at will and controlled the weather with great ease. The Jhinn were magical creatures who desired nothing more than to be left alone.

"Asnwaret mut Jhinn. Hemshaw conseshee emlar su Lilitu," she whispered.

The sky grew dark and black clouds rolled across the horizon as Lilith found herself surrounded by six Jhinn. They wore veils that concealed their faces and long flowing cloaks. Their dress appeared similar to the wandering nomads of the desert but was more colorful. The leader of the Jhinn slammed the end of his staff into the sand and lightning struck the ground at Lilith's feet.

"Why have you called us Lilith of Sumeria?" The Jhinn demanded.

"I have for you a proposal," Lilith said as she stood firmly in their midst.

"And what proposal could you offer us Lilith which we have not already heard? Why should we trust the one who was once a Sumerian Goddess herself?" The leader of the Jhinn hissed.

Lilith could see the Shinkar script that covered their skin as the dark clouds rolled across the sky above them and cast shadows upon their bodies.

"Because we have a common enemy. I believe you call him by the same name as I do. Enlil," Lilith whispered.

The sound of Enlil's name enraged Emsar and fire fell from the heavens. Eskrti, one of the younger Jhinn that accompanied Emsar, tossed his cape over Lilith to protect her. Lilith smiled at the young Jhinn who instantly averted his eyes. He was not used to kindness from such a beautiful woman.

"There is beauty in all creatures. Do not be afraid to look at me," Lilith whispered as she touched Eskrti's face.

Lilith noticed Erskti's skin was soft to her touch and appeared more human than that of the other Jhinn. Before she could speak to him again, Emsar grabbed Erskti by the arm forcefully and pulled him away from Lilith. Lilith did not understand why Emsar was so angered by her kindness toward Erskti.

"Do not treat him in that manner," Lilith said as she looked at Emsar disapprovingly.

"I will conduct matters which involve my children however I see fit," Emsar said angrily.

Lilith understood why the appearance of Erskti was so different than the other Jhinn who surrounded him. Erskti was a half-breed. He was part human.

"I offer you my sincerest apologies Emsar. I never desired to offend you. I was not aware he is your son. I thought the Jhinn were cursed the same as I have been, to never know the love of their own child," Lilith said.

"Walk with me Lilith and we shall discuss your proposal."

Lilith walked across the sand dunes of Sardis with Emsar until they came to a small oasis. He laid his cloak on the sand under the tall palm trees for Lilith. Emsar sat next to her and watched the soft waves on the water in front of them.

"To bear a child with a mortal is certain death for them. I loved my wife and was overjoyed when she told me she carried my child. I was the first Jhinn to bear a child with a mortal woman. I did not know my son would cause her life to end, or I would have never loved her."

The depth of Emsar's pain saddened Lilith as he sat next to her. He had loved his wife very deeply. It was not unlike a vampire and a mortal bearing a child. Any child conceived with an Immortal was a dangerous undertaking. Lilith pondered the possibilities of whether or not one of her children could bear the child of a Jhinn.

"I know what you are thinking Lilith. I do not believe it to be wise," Emsar said as he looked into her eyes.

"Have you ever seen one of my children in their true state? They are not so different than you and the other Jhinn. Would you not consider the possibility? I know there are women among my children who would find you to be beautiful."

The thought of being able to love another being the way he had loved his wife was enticing to Emsar. He also did not wish to condemn his son to a life of solitude the same as the other Jhinn.

"How would this even be remotely possible? No woman would willingly sacrifice themself to see if it were even possible," Jhinn replied.

"You are wrong Emsar. They would if I asked them to consider your proposal. We see the world differently than the other Immortals. For us, there is beauty in all life no matter what form it may take. To see the world through our eyes is to see the beauty no one else can see."

"We shall see. What has Enlil done to cause such anger in a woman as beautiful as you?" Emsar asked Lilith.

"My anger is complicated Emsar and the story long. I will not bore you with all the details. Suffice it to say he treats the Immortals like his slaves and the humans who surround us like they are Gods. He has made it his personal vendetta to punish me for creating my children because I used his precious humans to give my vampires life. My children, even though they were born through him, are no less important. I want for him to fall from the Heavens. Enlil must be taught a lesson."

"You would ask us to go to war with you?" Emsar asked.

"Yes."

"Then let there be war," Emsar said as he stood and offered Lilith his hand. "Call to you your supporters and I shall call the Jhinn. It has been many years since we stood in Heaven with Nergal against Enlil. This time we too are full-blooded Immortals. Our advantage will be much better that it was before. Have you lodging?"

Lilith shook her head no and then smiled. Emsar wrapped his arms around Lilith, and they disappeared beneath the sand. The world of the Jhinn existed beneath the great city of Sardis. It had been built from the stones and pillars left behind in the abandoned temples which had once graced the landscape just outside of Sardis. The city had a sensual feel to its nature. The Jhinn were much more complicated creatures than Lilith had been led to believe.

Lilith took note as she walked behind Emsar there were no women with the walls of the city. It was part of the curse Enlil had placed upon them. If they took a mortal bride, she would die in childbirth and only male Jhinn would ever be born.

Emsar's home was decorated lavishly. Warm hues of blues adorned the walls and richly woven tapestries hung from the walls. A portrait of a beautiful woman painted on camel skin hung in the entryway to his home. Lilith stopped to admire the painting.

"Your wife was lovely," Lilith whispered. "Erskti favors her."

Lilith wondered if the fact that his son resembled the boy's mother so greatly caused Emsar pain when he looked upon his son.

"Will you excuse me for one moment?" Lilith asked before she stepped into the other room. Emsar nodded his head as he tended to making a room ready for Lilith.

Lilith knew who would be the perfect companion for Emsar's son. Juel was a dark beauty who had come to be in Lilith's care many years ago. She was from the grassland fields of Sarmatia in the plains high above Sardis. Juel had been sold into slavery by the Romans when they raided her village. Juel had managed to escape the cruel Roman lord who owned her, and she fled to the city of Velch. Cassea had found her wandering the streets at night, badly beaten and barely able to walk.

At Lilith's request, Cassea embraced her. In the thirty years she had resided with Lilith, Juel had never embraced another or chosen to bond. Her heart belonged to Sarmatia she had once told Lilith and until she found a Sarmatian man she would love no other. Lilith closed her eyes and called to Juel. She told her to come to her in Sardis. Juel appeared before Lilith as Emsar entered the room. Just as Lilith was about to explain the situation to Juel, Erskti appeared next to his father. His veil did not cover his face. Juel gasped as she placed her fingers to her lips.

"Jhinn," Juel whispered.

Erskti quickly pulled the veil across his face to conceal his appearance. Juel was not afraid of Erskti. Instead, she was only startled. She had believed the tales of the Jhinn to be only a myth used to scare children. Juel floated gracefully across the floor toward Erskti, placing her hands on his back as he turned away from her. She unfastened the veil and allowed it to fall to the floor by her feet as she unwound the linen that hid him from the outside world. As Erskti's long black hair fell from beneath the linen wrappings, Juel brushed Erskti's hair away from his face as she leaned forward so she could see his eyes and smiled at him.

Erskti was shy and inexperienced. He trembled as Juel touched him. Erskti had been warned many times that it was forbidden for a Jhinn to love a mortal woman. He was confused by her gentle touch and why she was not afraid of him. Juel knew she had found the love she had waited for and was not afraid. She found him to be beautiful. Juel kissed him softly on the cheek before returning to Lilith's side. Lilith knew Juel was already enamored with the handsome son of Emsar.

"This is one of my many children. She came to me as a slave many years ago. She is the vampire called Juel. I believe she has already introduced herself to your son," Lilith said as she smiled at Emsar.

Emsar motioned to Lilith to follow him into the adjoining room.

"She does not fear him," Emsar whispered.

"Juel is Sarmatian. She knows the many legends which surround the Jhinn. She will make Erskti a fine wife. She will bear him a strong son," Lilith said confidently.

Lilith and Emsar returned to the other room to find Juel sitting next to Esrkti on the many large pillows which covered the floor. She was telling him about her life and the soft sweeping grasslands from whence she came. Juel told him about what had happened to her at the hands of her captors when they took her to Rome. Erskti's heart filled with sadness as Juel told him about what they had done to her and touched her face.

"I would never harm you," he whispered.

Juel closed her eyes at his touch. Lilith sighed as she watched the two young lovers together before Emsar led her from his home into the street.

"She cares for him already. How is this possible? Did you enchant her so she would love my son?" Emsar asked.

"Love knows to whom it belongs without the intervention of any woman or any man. Juel has always been kind and loving. In all the time she has resided in my home, she has taken no lover to her bed. She told me her heart and her love were reserved for a man she had not yet met from her homeland. I knew in my heart it was Erskti she was meant to love when I looked into his eyes. He has the same soulful, sad, eyes as my Juel."

"Perhaps, Lilith, this arrangement will be fruitful for us both. You have not told me how you wish to draw Enlil out. Have you devised a plan?" Emsar asked as he stood next to Lilith.

"If we were simply to kill his beloved humans, then his wrath would be great and would be focused upon us alone. So I have decided to use the world around us to kill his humans, together we will create violent storms, horrendous quakes shall shake the ground, and blood shall run from the mountains. He will come to look for me, for Enlil will know it is me who is responsible for the mayhem that has befallen his humans. This is when I will exact my revenge. I wish to tie him to the Tree of Woe just the same as he did me."

"Lilith, what you ask is no easy task. Capturing a supreme God is difficult."

"I will use one of his pet humans as bait. He will intercede if he believes I will kill her. Amarla has been a favorite of his for many years now. He will do whatever is necessary to save her."

Lilith turned into a wisp of smoke and appeared in the House of Set. Astarte was reclined across Set's lap as he fed her grapes. The worship of Egyptian Gods was coming to its end but Set still held power and had many followers. He did not have to go into hiding as many of the other Gods had chosen to do.

"Mother, you honor me with your presence. It has been many years," Set said as he maneuvered from beneath Astarte who smiled at Lilith.

"I have come to seek a favor. I need to kidnap a woman who resides in the land of the Hittites. Her name is Amarla."

Set stretched his mighty black wings behind him and then stretched them out at his sides, casting shadows upon the marble floor.

"Where would you like this woman delivered?" Set asked as he approached his mother.

"I want her crucified on the Tree of Woe."

Set lowered his wings, wrapping them around himself as he contemplated her words.

"What you ask is a dangerous undertaking. What is this woman to you?" Set asked.

"She is the consort of Enlil on Earth," Lilith replied dryly.

"Mother, you must not continue to anger him." Set was concerned his Mother continued upon a path of vengeance that would result in her demise.

"Child, he cannot kill me for I was the first born. I only wish to punish him. He toys in matters not his affairs. He has set a traitor amongst the Firenzean Vampires. I cannot allow his behavior to continue."

"As you wish," Set whispered and disappeared.

Lilith sat next Astarte and took her hand.

"When Set returns, you must leave this place and go to the Underworld and dwell with Nergal. It will be the only safe place for you as I fight Enlil. I know him too well, and he will seek out all that I love and destroy it. You must promise me Astarte, you must give me your solemn word."

"I will take Set to the Hall of Nergal."

Lilith was pleased her son would be safe. She turned her attention toward the arrival of Amarla and the destruction of Enlil.

When Set returned with Amarla, he tossed her at Lilith's feet. She trembled in her presence.

"Please do not hurt me. I beg of you," Amarla pleaded.

"You are a mortal and lay with a God. Have you no shame? Have you no sense of your importance?" Lilith asked.

Amarla was confused by Lilith's words. She did not understand what Lilith was implying.

"Your body is your own. He has no right to it solely because he is a God."

"But he loves me," Amarla whispered.

"You are more a fool than I could have hoped for. Do you honestly believe he loves you? Let me tell you about the beautiful Enlil. His breath is full of lies and is sweet like honey nectar. He will weave his web of lies around you until you allow your guard to drop, then he will take from you until he tires of your beauty. Then he will seek another. You will be but one of his many conquests and will matter no more."

Lilith stood and her eyes glowed an ominous red as she looked down at the shivering woman at her feet.

"Take her to the Tree. I shall crucify her myself," Lilith commanded. Set wrapped his arms around Amarla and disappeared.

Lilith appeared next to the Tree of Woe and was filled with anger as she remembered the cruel treatment Enlil had forced her to endure. She slid her hand down the face of the large cypress and looked to the skies above her as she smiled.

Lilith took the iron spikes that had once held her body to the tree and drove them through Amarla's hands and feet. Amarla screamed out in pain as Lilith drove the spikes in slowly. When she had finished, she turned toward her son.

"Go now to Emsar and bid him to begin the devastation. Return to your home and take Astarte to Nergal's lair and do not return until I call you. Tell Emsar I may need his aid again."

Set disappeared to do his Mother's bidding. Lilith sat at the base of the tree and awaited Enlil's arrival. Emsar set into motion the devastation Lilith requested with his might staff. He called storms to flood the plains, the mountains spewed forth luminous fire, and the Earth shook violently. Lilith called devastation to her midst and unleashed plagues of grasshoppers to destroy the crops Enlil's humans so carefully tended. As Enlil tended to his humans, Lilith took delight.

A week had passed since Set had abducted Amarla. Lilith cared for her, giving her water and food as she hung from the Tree of Woe. Lilith provided her with comfort and shade from the searing mid-day sun, a luxury which Lilith was not given when she had hung upon the Tree.

At the end of the second week, Enlil still had not come to retrieve his beloved Amarla. So Lilith called to Juel and bid her to embrace his beloved. At the end of the second week, Amarla was human no more. Lilith took Amarla with her and waited by the Dead Sea for Enlil's arrival. She was disappointed in his lack of concern for the woman he pretended to love. Lilith knew she would not be able to lure him to the Tree of Woe. She would have to seek out another way to punish him.

His anger was fierce as he appeared behind Lilith. Enlil knew he could not anger An and Ki by hurting Lilith.

"What have you done to her?" Enlil demanded.

"I only improved on what you began. Do you not find her beautiful? I do." Lilith laughed as she felt his hot breath against the back of her neck.

"Who aids you in the destruction of them?" Enlil took Lilith forcefully by the shoulders and spun her around to face him.

"Your cruel treatment of others has left you little in the way of supporters. You now have more enemies than friends in the world of Immortals. How does that make you feel Enlil? You made yourself so superior you ostracized yourself from all those who would love you."

Lilith stood before Enlil. It was the first time she could remember where there was no love in her heart for him. He had taken from her the ability to feel empathy and she no longer cared.

"What has happened to you Lilith?" Enlil asked.

Lilith was not coy in her reply. She meant the single word she said to him.

"You," Lilith replied.

"You have become wicked and heartless. This is not the Lilith I know. Where has your desire for love gone?"

"You took that from me long ago. Know this, Enlil, this war between us is not over. I will never stop. I will continue to haunt you through all time. I will continue to use whatever methods are at my disposal to make you suffer just the same as you have done to me. In the end, when there is only the two of us that remains, it will not be me that comforts you. You will be alone, and perhaps, then you will understand what you have done."

Lilith disappeared, leaving Enlil alone with the newly born vampire Amarla. Enlil in his disgust at Amarla's condition, thrust his hand into her chest and pulled out her heart. Amarla burst into flames and crumbled to ash as Enlil wept at the edge of the Dead Sea.

Chapter Thirteen
The Gift of the Seal

It became evident if Lilith was to win the battle she fought against Enlil she would need an ally, one who was close to her former love whom she could trust implicitly. This ally would also need to be one who had lost favor in Enlil's eyes and sought a way to reclaim it.

For many years Lilith scoured the desert sands of her home and surrounding countryside searching for such a man until she came to the fallen town of Masada; here lied a castle in ruins awaiting a King, and Lilith knew just the King she wished to put there.

A single human held the captive eye of Enlil, one who worshipped him above all others. Lilith knew all too well the hearts of men and how easily they could be swayed with the whispers of power and glory. She set out to locate the man who would become her pawn and continued crusade against Enlil.

She stood in the shadows listening for the name of the man whose greatness preceded him until she reached the outskirts of Masada. It was then she heard his name and began her quest to capture his attention.

Suleiman was known to be a devout man, but just like all humans, he was weak. His flaws laid in many areas but none so great as his penchant for the softness of female flesh. In his house, he kept seven hundred wives and three hundred concubines. It was rumored that none of them were the true object of his desire. She was the leverage Lilith needed to secure his devotion to her. Lilith would bring to Suleiman the most prized woman in all of Babylon and Sumer, or Egypt; the Queen of Sheba. The only woman who was so brazen as to rebuke his advances and deny him entry to her golden city was known to the world as the Queen of Sheba, but to Lilith she was known as Aswani. She was no stranger to Lilith or to her son Set. She was one of his many concubines and was a vampire.

Lilith appeared in the gilded central hall of the Queen's palace whose arched ceilings contained murals of the forgotten Sumerian Gods. The sprawling white wings of Inanna swept across the central portion of the mural and were tinged in gold. Only a human who had seen Inanna in person could have painted such a fine depiction of her. Lilith smiled slightly as she remembered the kindness Inanna had once shone her.

Her unannounced appearance was not without notice. Lilith soon found herself surrounded by the palace guard. When they gazed upon her, they immediately fell at her feet in submission. Aswani called to Lilith upon seeing her. Her heart was glad. It had been many moons in passing since she had seen the one to whom she owed the grandeur of her life.

"Lilith of Sumeria, what brings you to my palace?"

"I have come to seek a favor of you, Aswani. It would appear one who is enamored with you could be of benefit to me in the war I rage. I hoped, perhaps, you would be willing to aid me."

Aswani dismissed the guard knowing that what Lilith was about to reveal could be heard by no one but her.

"There is a certain King who desires your affections. Should you be able to arrange a liaison with this King, I could weave myself into his company and secure what I must."

Aswani walked alongside Lilith as she listened to her words until they reached the Garden of Amiah. The sweet scent of heliotrope filled the air around them as Lilith made known her wishes.

"I wish for you to make an alliance with King Suleiman."

"Suleiman? But why?"

"He is the favored one of Enlil. I should like to see him become my pawn."

Her words were enough. She did not need to convince Aswani any further. In the morning, she would send an emissary to the King of Masada and begin weaving her web of treachery.

An entire moon passed before King Suleiman sent word to the Queen of Sheba that he would welcome her presence in his court. Lilith made the preparations for her arrival to be an extravagant one. Her procession was led by twelve white stallions draped in golden cloth, twenty acrobats, fourteen chariots carrying chests filled with jewels and gold, and thirteen concubines for the King to add to his collection. The Queen herself was carried in a crimson and gold carriage on the backs of six men. When she arrived at the gate to Masada, King Suleiman was there to welcome her.

Masada was but an infant compared to the cities that surrounded her and did not yet have the splendor of a thriving kingship. The court and the King were housed in a palace of meager proportions compared to the Queen of Sheba. She was polite in her mannerisms though disappointed at his lack of wealth. Her face was obscured from his view, which disappointed the King. He had heard many stories of the grand nature of her beauty. King Suleiman had hoped to behold that beauty with his own eyes upon her arrival. He offered the Queen his hand as she stepped from her carriage.

"So small a kingdom you have for such a King with a great reputation," Aswani said, smiling beneath her veil. Tormenting him would be an act she would enjoy greatly.

"I have yet to procure a kingdom as rich and diverse as yours, great Queen. It is my hope one day to have one as such. Until then, I must make do with what God has provided me."

"You are a man of faith?" The Queen asked as she walked with him inside the palace gate.

"I am a man of many faiths, all of which I hope to use to gain fame and glory. What of your beliefs, great Queen, to whom do you honor with your fortunate life?"

"I do not wish to discuss such matters. I did not come here to discuss religious philosophy with you. I worship but one God, the Sun God, and no other."

The Queen of Sheba stayed with King Suleiman for many days during which he made known his amorous intentions toward the beautiful and young Queen. Every aspect of her intrigued him from the soft scent of heliotrope she wore to the way the sun illuminated her hair like burnt cinnamon. Despite his wit and charm, King Suleiman could not charm the royal bounty from beneath the robes she wore. The King was reduced to near begging at the prospect of bedding her but Aswani refused. Instead, she proposed that if he could answer three questions, then she would readily give him the royal bounty.

King Suleiman, who believed himself wise and educated, believed this would be a simple task. There were, after all, only three questions. Aswani, knowing the conceit of the King, fashioned her questions in the form of complex riddles.

"Were a man to request the aid of the Gods, what manner of the master of the elements must he abide?" Aswani asked.

"Your riddle is a simple one. Any man must know that in order to master the elements, one must bless the water, then abstain from all that is vile, idle, and vain, fast and be vigil and recite prayer five times before laying down to sleep."

The Queen of Sheba had not expected King Suleiman to know the answer so quickly being he professed himself to be the follower of one God. It was now apparent to her that he knew more about the ways of the old Gods than he willing admitted. She would have to choose her next riddle with much more consideration.

"Name for me the thirty-five archangels," Aswani replied.

"This is where you are mistaken, great Queen, for in the Heavens above there are but thirty-four archangels," Suleiman replied with confidence.

Aswani, being clever in the wording of her riddle, began to laugh.

"I never said in the Heavens above you. You forget the one who fell from grace. Even he is still an archangel, just of another realm."

Suleiman frowned at her in his disgust. She had outwitted him.

"Tell me then, what is the composition of gold?"

"That is a secret which I am not able to reveal. I fear I have failed your test."

"Being that I am a gracious Queen, I will grant you one more. Should you answer this one correctly, then I shall give to you the royal bounty."

"Who was the first woman?"

"That is easy. She was Lilith," Suleiman answered with even more confidence than he had her prior questions. When he said her name, Lilith stepped from the shadows, forced open his hand, and placed on his finger a ring.

"Your royal bounty," Lilith said smiling.

Suleiman realizing the nature of the trickery surrounding him slammed his fist into the table and pointed at the Queen of Sheba.

"I said royal bounty. I never said my bounty."

"What is this trinket you have given me?" Suleiman questioned as he examined the ring.

"It is the Seal of Suleiman. It is your desire to be a King with wealth and means. This ring shall give you command over realms unseen. You will be imparted with great wisdom, favor, and powers not known to the world of man. I shall also grant to you a friendship that will be of great benefit to you, for I know the words of the Jhinn and can bring them to you. They shall show you the hidden glory of the world that is not accessible to other humans. I will reward you with riches, a glorious reign not known before by any other King. You shall rule not only man and beast but also demons, spirits, and other ethereal beings. Masada will grow beyond what you imagined, and you shall oversee it all."

"What must I give to you, Lilith of Sumeria, in exchange for this bounty? Is it my soul you desire?" King Suleiman asked.

Lilith's laughter echoed through the hall.

"Simple human, do you believe I would have use for something as trivial as your soul? I ask for an article much greater than your soul. I ask for your loyalty. I do not ask you to turn away from your God or to make sacrifice to me. I ask that in return for what I have bestowed upon you, you remember where your loyalties lie."

"Your trickery is superlative for I knew not that which I desired would never be mine to attain."

Aswani stood as she began to unbutton the robe which covered her gown. "To you I never said I would deny my bounty. I mere said the royal bounty was not what you believed."

When the Queen of Sheba reached the door that led from the room, a trail of clothing laid on the floor behind her. Lilith sat in the throne of King Suleiman and patiently awaited their return. Once Suleiman and the Queen had satisfied their lust, they rejoined Lilith in the central hall of the palace.

"Now that you have the seal, I will tell you what your loyalty will mean to me and how it will benefit you. You will stay in favor with Enlil. You will honor him above all others. Yet you will also supply me with any and all information I ask for in regards to your God. I shall, in return, teach you how to use the seal. You will grow wealthy in riches and power. Your kingdom will become renowned for its advancement. I will grow wealthy in the knowledge I seek. To compliment your Kingship, I shall offer you the consul of the Jhinn for as long as they feel you are worthy of their attention. You will become the King of Kings."

Suleiman contemplated Lilith's words carefully. There was not one thing he desired more than becoming an all-powerful King. Suleiman extended his hand to Lilith.

"We have an accord."

Aswani remained with Suleiman for only part of the year each year. Suleiman continued to honor Enlil, who for his dedication and faith, granted him the gift of wisdom. Masada grew into a fabled city with exotic spices, the finest woven cloth, and superior work in all metals both known to man and to the Gods. His logic and wisdom was sought by many, including kings from outside his reign. Even the Pharaohs of Egypt paid homage to Suleiman and his wise rule, offering him horses, chariots, and wives out of respect. Lilith was pleased as she watched his destiny unfold by her hand. Through Suleiman, Lilith could learn the inner workings of Enlil's daily life. She knew eventually Enlil would seek the wisdom of his exalted human. When he did, Lilith would be waiting in the shadows to collect her price.

Suleiman, with his great wealth and prosperity, built a temple like none other seen. It stood high above the land with a domed cap layered in gold. In the dome stood an observatory where his astrologers mapped the stars and planned the King's destiny through their movement. Through the actions of his astrologers and the gift of the Seal, Suleiman commanded not only Heaven and Earth but also what lied below. He soon learned that being a King of such wealth and power came with a cost. Enemies abounded who desired to steal from Suleiman the sacred seal which Lilith had given him. As a gift for the information Suleiman readily supplied to Lilith, she brought to him a Shamir, a sacred and magical worm known only to the Jhinn. He aided Suleiman in building his many temples by raising the stones and cleaving them with the touch of his tail. From that moment forward, King Suleiman pledged his undying allegiance to Lilith and his fate was sealed.

Lilith was able to learn much about Enlil she did not know from her conversations with Suleiman. His weakness for his beloved humans was even greater than Lilith had realized. He also spoke of a Goddess with whom he was at war to Suleiman but never divulged her name. He told Suleiman he was about to unleash an unbridled devastation upon the one whom this Goddess loved above all others. Lilith knew time was now her foe. She had little time to make use of what she had learned.

Chapter Fourteen
Mayhem Abounds

Lilith returned to Emsar and bade him to stop. She had begun what she wanted and could continue the last on her own. She remained with Emsar and the Jhinn for several years as the love between Erskti and Juel blossomed. For their wedding, Lilith gave Juel a large ruby broach. Only a month after their wedding, Juel was already with child. Emsar was fearful for her condition and pleaded with Lilith to remain until the child was born.

The birth was a difficult one for Juel, being the child was the result of an Immortal. After many hours of labor, Juel presented Erskti with a beautiful daughter. Emsar pledged his loyalty to Lilith for all eternity at his joy over the birth of the child; who was beautiful the same as Juel with a faint hint of blue cast to her skin. They called the child Larah. Her eyes were like lipid pools of blue spring-water.

Though Emsar pleaded with Lilith to stay with him, she refused. Emsar had grown fond of Lilith and desired for her to stay and become his wife.

"I am honored but must respectfully say no. It is not that I do not care for you. It is I cannot love you for my heart belongs to another. One day I shall see him again and walk within his crimson halls."

Emsar knew Lilith spoke of Nergal. The Jhinn had stood with Nergal on the battlefield when the first war began after Enlil cursed them, and he had given rites to their dead. Emsar had stood in the crimson halls of the Wargod when he buried his wife. He understood Lilith's position. He knew she must return to her love and her children. "Keep vigil over Suleiman for me."

Lilith appeared in the Catacombs of the Firenzea to find Cassea faithfully tending those who dwelt there.

"I am pleased you have returned," Cassea said as she knelt before Lilith.

"Where is Lucius?" Lilith asked.

"He is now a Senator and has many followers, though I believe it is out of fear by which they follow him and not respect. Marcus Aurelius introduced Lucius to a woman and her companions only a day before your return this day. It is whispered she is the Queen of our kind, but how could this be?"

"She is your Queen, child, just as I am the Mother of the Vampire race. I gave to her a piece of me when I created her. She is one of six vampires in existence who could withstand my kiss. She is perfection among my children, just as are her friends. They are pure and perfect in every way. You should respect her as such."

Cassea noticed the change in Lilith's demeanor as she spoke and immediately apologized.

"Do not be angry with me, I did not know." Cassea knelt at Lilith's feet.

"I am not angry with you Cassea. You could not have known her importance. Come now, do not cry. I am never angry with my children." Lilith knelt to wipe her tears.

"Come, I would like to see Petronius and visit the Roman baths. Today is a day to rejoice, for she has come back to me."

Lilith could not have known that Enlil watched her from afar, plotting his revenge for the embrace of Amarla as she rejoiced with the many vampires of Firenzea.

Lilith grew to love the Roman baths and built above it a home that was luxurious. She conducted all manners of business and settled all quarrels within the walls of her bathhouse as she kept a watchful eye on Ari from afar. Aranthe had returned to Velch, and all was peaceful for a time. Lilith grew content in her life as Aranthe and found a small amount of happiness surrounded by the Firenzean Clan.

Enlil watched carefully for the precise moment to intervene, and appeared to Lucius as a luminous swan in his garden and spoke to him.

"You must kill the daughter if you want revenge for your father's death Lucius."

Lucius was frightened by the swan and that it could speak, but as he approached the swan it shifted into Enlil, who then sat on the stone wall of the pond as he looked at Lucius.

"You are an Immortal," Lucius whispered as he approached Enlil cautiously.

"If revenge is what you seek, then you must strike her where she is weakest. You must kill her daughter. Do this and I shall grant you true immortality."

Enlil vanished. The seeds of treachery were planted. Now all Enlil had to do was wait and watch patiently for his plan to unfold. By crushing Lilith's beloved creation, Enlil felt he could break her, once and for all. Enlil did not understand nor could he see the depth of how Lilith had hardened herself because of his actions. It would not turn out has he planned.

It took nearly a month for Lucius to enact his revenge. Before that time came, Ari visited Lilith at the bathhouse with Uriah as her protector. Lilith was enamored with Uriah for reasons she could reveal to Ari. She knew that in the end, Uriah would be the one who would comfort her most beautiful creation.

Lilith knew about Enlil's plan, yet she did not intervene. It was not her place to lay judgment upon the vampires of the world, that task belonged to their Queen alone. In her anger, the vampire Lilith loved above all others vowed she would never speak to Lilith again.

Lilith in her sorrow plotted one last great attack against Enlil, but to do this she would need all the forgotten Gods of the Heavens to take her side.

Lilith went first to Enuki, the trickster and explained to him her plans. She desired for Enuki to trick Enlil into believing Lilith was remorseful for her behavior regarding Amarla and desired a truce.

Lilith then called Mes Lam Taea, the war aspect of her beloved Nergal to take over him and bring him to her from the crimson cavern in Kur, the Underworld, to head her war. Sara also agreed to take part in what they were about to create as he despised Enlil and his desire for peace. Erra called the Sebitti who had long been removed from the carnage and war they were known to create and desired to make once more. Now Lilith had to convince one more God to help her, Lugal Irra, the Lord of Plagues.

When Mes Lam Taea appeared before Lilith in his splendor, fully dressed in Sumerian Armor, with a double edged mace in both hands, Lilith danced around him.

"So strong, so virile," Lilith whispered as she slid her hands down Mes Lam Taea's massive arms. "Incite within them the desire for war, give them a reason to fight, and let them kill each other one by one."

"Sara, fill their heads with lies, turning man against man. I will give you the carnage you desire. Blood will cover the land that was once our home. They will fight to the death to own a piece of insignificant dirt that is meaningless, all created by the lies will lay."

"Erra and Sebitti, I can give you the brutality and lust for conquest you desire."

"What will you do Lilith when this all is happening?" Sara asked.

"I shall join the fight and kill as many as I am able. First, I must ensure that Enlil believes I am remorseful and wish to fight with him no more. Then I will unleash my anger and the humans will beg for mercy as they clamor at my feet. Then I shall call one last Goddess to fight amongst us. I will call Tiamat."

Lilith listened closely to the whispers of the Gods who surrounded her. Tiamat was uncontrollable and volatile, unpredictable and complete desolation. The Gods were afraid of Tiamat and her powers. She controlled legions of followers and could call fearsome beasts from the seas. Tiamat embodied all that was beautiful to Lilith. Tiamat was strong, independent, and allowed no other God to control her.

"Quiet your thoughts. Tiamat can rule the seas like no other. Who better to aid us on this journey?" Lilith asked.

"She is not one of us," the Sebitti whispered in unison.

"The Gods are known by many names. Who is to say she is not but one of the many manifestations we have held throughout the centuries. Nergal himself is known by many names, each a different attribute as is desired by the one who calls to him. Those who have been loyal to us, the Gods of old, they shall not be punished, but the humans who have remained loyal to Enlil and followed him in his many guises, those will be the ones who shall suffer. Do you hold no anger in your heart toward them for how insignificant they have made us? We were the first Gods. We inhabited this world long before they were created. Is it not time we took back what has belonged to us all along?"

Lilith incited anger within the other Gods as they thought about how they had fallen from favor with the humans because of Enlil's actions. They once stood in the Hall of the Gods and held the same importance as Enlil. Now they were but faint memories in the hearts of a few loyal humans who had passed the stories of the Gods down throughout the centuries and kept them alive in their hearts.

"I stood in Atlantis and brought down the mighty city when they failed to honor the Gods as they should at the request of their Gods. Tiamat and I stood side by side with the Atlantian Gods and called forth the oceans to swallow their island and sink it to the bottom of the sea. We are all powerful. We can defeat him."

The Sebitti were the first Gods to step forward, followed by Erra, Mes An Du, and Sara. Belet-Seri appeared next to Lilith, her tablet in hand as she began to scribe the names of those who would perish as she called them to their deaths. The circle of devastation was complete. Lilith surrounded herself with the most powerful Gods of the old world.

Now, Lilith knew she would have to focus on her seduction of Enlil. She left the other Gods to plot their revenge. Lilith readied herself to confront the one who had caused all the rage and sorrow that filled her being.

Lilith appeared in the Heavens and awaited Enlil to discover she stood on his ground and not her own. Her lips were as red as rubies, her eyes glowed a soft shade of lavender, and her black hair glistened as it softly swayed to and fro across her back as she ascended the stairway that led to the Hall of the Gods. The long train of her black gown danced behind her as the wind followed her up the staircase.

Lilith came to the door that led Enlil's Court, a Court now presided over by Enlil alone. Though An and Ki's presence could still be felt, they were now the Supreme Gods who oversaw the universe and no longer oversaw the lessor Gods of man. Lilith lifted the great lion-headed knocker and allowed it to slip from her fingers. The sound of thunder rumbled across the Heavens as Lilith waited for Enlil to arrive.

The door to the Hall of the Gods parted and a golden fog rolled across the floor toward Lilith until it surrounded her. The mist caressed Lilith as she awaited Enlil. Lilith attempted to be patient as she awaited him. She could not appear to have motive. Lilith knew she needed to create the perfect illusion of sincerity, so she thought about Nergal and how much she loved him.

Lilith laid down upon the stairs and fell asleep as she awaited Enlil's arrival. Enlil did not trust Lilith, with good reason, so he allowed her to linger. If she was not honest in her intentions, then Enlil believed that if he caused her great delay, Lilith would become angered and reveal her true intentions.

Lilith awoke, surrounded by the same golden mist but with one exception. Enlil sat next to her upon the stairs. Lilith wondered how long he had been there watching her as she slept.

"Why are you here Lilith?" Enlil asked.

"I have come to ask for your forgiveness. It was wrong of me to take Amarla away from you. It is obvious that you cared for her deeply. I am a woman as well as a Goddess. When our hearts are hurt, we often strike out at those we love. It was my way of punishing you for your indiscretions. Did you not once love me? What did I do to cause you to stop?" Lilith asked as she feigned tears of remorse.

Enlil moved closer to Lilith. For the first time in the many years he had known her, he was able to see how his behavior had hurt her. Lilith used the magic of Ningirama to weave a spell around Enlil's heart and cause him to feel empathy for her.

"I became obsessed with the power the other Gods allowed me. I could not see the injustice I did to you. You were a pawn to me, a force I thought I could manipulate to do my will, but I quickly learned that your will was greater, stronger than mine. This angered me greatly."

"It is not wrong for a woman to have free will or to refuse to be subservient. It is not wrong for a woman to be able to think freely and have her own desires that need satisfied." Lilith paused before she placed her hand against

Enlil's cheek. "Did I not once fill you with desire and satisfy you as no other could?" Lilith whispered.

Her breath was sweet like summer flowers as she whispered in Enlil's ear. He was captivated by the mystique she presented. Enlil pulled Lilith's hand from his face and held it tightly in his.

"Stay with me Lilith, here, in the Hall of Gods and be my Queen."

Lilith knew if she agreed she would place herself in great danger without a way to escape. Enlil could easily overpower her with his size or with his gaze.

"Would you have asked me a thousand years ago, I would have fallen at your feet, but I cannot. I cannot betray the love I feel for your son. I love Nergal above all others. One day hope to return to him," Lilith said as she slowly removed her hand from Enlil's grasp.

"Are there no words I can say to convince you to stay with me Lilith?"

"I ask only for your forgiveness and that I might stay with you for a while so that we may put the days of being enemies behind us."

Lilith heard Enlil sigh and knew that the spell Ningirama had woven was weaving its way around Enlil and making him sympathetic toward her.

Enlil stood and offered Lilith his hand.

"Then stay with me, Lilith of Sumeria, not as my enemy but as my friend."

Lilith placed her hand in Enlil's as she stood and then followed him inside the gilded doors to the Hall of the Gods. As Lilith walked down the corridor that led to the courtroom, she gazed as her surroundings with a sense of wonder and awe. It had been nearly seven thousand years since Lilith had walked in the Hall of the Gods. Lilith had forgotten the splendor it held.

Enlil called for a great feast to be held in Lilith's honor and took her to her room to prepare for the evening's festivities. Enlil opened the door to Lilith's room and waited as she entered.

"What is this?" Lilith asked as she looked around the room. It was decorated rather lavishly with golden statues of her winged lions, a large bed covered in dark purple linen, and golden harp in the corner of the room.

"It is for you. I have kept it for you all these years in the event you returned home," Enlil said and then closed the door behind him, leaving Lilith alone to contemplate his offer to remain with him.

In the corner of the room was a lavender gown with royal purple trim and gold threads woven into the edges that lay over the chair, which sat in front of the harp. Lilith felt the fabric. She thought it felt like air it was woven so finely. She thought about whether or not she had been too hard on Enlil over the years. Perhaps his power had overwhelmed him as a new God. Perhaps he knew not what he had done. As Lilith continued to look around the room, she found it to be filled with items that reminded her of every cruel act Enlil had committed against her. Her sympathy for Enlil quickly faded as Lilith dressed for the gala that awaited her.

Lilith braided her hair and swept it into a conical bun, allowing several strands of her hair to cascade down from the center. She fastened the amethyst necklace around her neck and admired the craftsmanship of the silver the stones were set in before she stood to join Enlil in the dining hall. As Lilith walked down the long hall that led to the dining room, she prayed her accomplices were busy at work making war.

Mes An Du and Erra led the war in the Middle East and incited within man the desire to fight. Mes Lam Taea stood high atop the mountain as his warlike manner infected the humans in Germania and caused Arminius to revolt against the Roman Army to which he had once pledged his allegiance. The Sebitti divided into pairs and traveled together inciting war in Parthia and Armenia, but they were not yet finished for they had not yet called Tiamat into the battle.

Tiamat appeared before Lilith as she gracefully floated along the corridor.

"They are beautiful when they fight," Tiamat whispered.

"You have done well my sister. I shall remain with Enlil and occupy his thoughts, allowing you to do what you do best, my lovely Tiamat."

Tiamat disappeared. Lilith continued to walk slowly to the dining hall. Once she reached the hall, Lilith was greeted by Enlil who was dressed all in white, wearing a long tunic embroidered with angelic script that reminded Lilith of the beautiful enchanted script of the Jhinn.

The table was nearly the length of the hall, stretching forty foot from one end of the hall to the other. Wines from the imperial vineyards of the Romans graced the table. A large roasted boar sat upon a silver platter decorated with sugared plums and spiced apples. Enlil appeared next to Lilith and handed her the golden chalice from her place setting. As she lifted the chalice to her lips, she could smell the blood inside and knew it was Enlil's. Lilith replaced the chalice on the table and smiled at Enlil as she took her place at the table.

They spoke little as they ate, and Enlil observed that Lilith had not yet drank from her chalice, which angered him slightly. If Lilith meant the words she had spoken, then she should not refuse him in this manner.

"Are you not thirsty Lilith? Is it not to your liking?" Enlil asked coyly.

"I am afraid I cannot partake of what you have placed her for me. I cannot take the blood of a God other than the one I love. I do not love you Enlil. I wish only for us to no longer be enemies."

Lilith knew if she consumed Enlil's blood she would have no power against him. Enlil could possibly take her power from her then all would be lost. She smiled softly at Enlil as he stared at her. His deception had failed. Lilith's deception was now well underway.

Chapter Fifteen
The Resurrection of Tiamat

Tiamat appeared before the other Gods as they gathered to reunite in Kur. She was a striking beauty in her own right, though her beauty was different and much darker than Lilith's. Tiamat's long black gown clung to her body as she stood before them. Her long, dark, red hair was like molten fire as it danced on the wind. The other Gods backed away from her as she walked toward Mes Lam Taea. Tiamat stopped before him. She circled him before she paused to lay her hands upon his broad shoulders.

"To what honor am I granted your presence, great Sumerian God of War, pestilence, death, and destruction?"

Tiamat was enamored with Mes Lam Taea and his reputation among the Sumerian Gods.

"There is no honor to be spoken of Tiamat. I am present at the request of the one to whom my heart belongs," Mes Lam Taea said coldly as he pulled Tiamat's hands from his shoulders.

Tiamat sighed as she walked away from Mes Lam Taea and approached Lugal Irra.

"You smell of death and plague, how delightful," Tiamat whispered as she passed him. She stopped before Mes An Du, whose brilliance nearly blinded her.

"And you, you are the brilliant rays used to blind them in battle so they may not see whom they fight."

The Sebitti formed a circle around Erra and blocked Tiamat from coming into contact with him as she stood in front of Erra. Erra felt no fear and broke through the barrier they formed and offered his hand to Tiamat.

"Perhaps, Great Goddess, if you were to indulge us with your legend they would not be so fearful of you," Erra said as he took Tiamat's hand.

Tiamat motioned toward the throne, which stood in the corner of room that had once been the throne of Ereskigal. The chair slid effortless across the floor to where Tiamat stood. She pulled the long fabric of her dress to the side before she sat.

"I am desolation. I am chaos. I give birth to dragons and sea serpents only to please myself. I have no love for any other God nor the human race. I am Tiamat. What more is there to know?" Tiamat asked as she reclined against the back of the throne.

"Surely, Great Goddess, there is more to you than chaos," Erra said as he approached Tiamat and sat next to her. Tiamat smiled slightly. It had been many years since her creation had been told.

"I am chaos, the energy from whence the world came. I am the primordial darkness from whence your Lilith was born. She and I are the same in many ways. I slept until they tore me in two in order to create the world beneath our feet. For this were they grateful? Did they offer me sacrifice? No, for this they murdered my children and caused me to take on the form of a great sea serpent."

All the Gods were silent as Tiamat spoke, listening intently to her words as she wove the tale of her existence and demise.

"My children were beautiful creatures but the other Gods feared them, especially Ea. Your Enlil reminds me much of Ea, infantile, conceited, and full of envy. He bade Marduk to kill me, and so he did."

"Might I inquire why you should take Lilith's cause as your own?" Mes Lam Taea asked as he stepped forward.

"Your Enlil, he is my great grandson. Your Lilith, she is my sister. I existed long before the names of the Gods were even known to man. An and Ki are my children.

It saddens me that they would so willingly relinquish their place among the Gods to become but a whisper. I allowed Marduk to kill me, in theory, so that Enlil could create his beautiful world, but had I known this is what would happen, I would have killed Marduk when the opportunity presented itself. I too have a weakness for Enlil, the same as Lilith, but for his disobedience, I do not. Lilith is much older than Enlil, nearly as old as I." Tiamat laughed, and her laughter shook the ground beneath her.

"How can this be so?" Mes Lam Taea asked as he crossed his arms in disbelief.

"When An and Ki were but babes in the sense of the word, they pulled Lilith from the primordial darkness where she slept with me. The manner in which my children conducted themselves did not please me, especially the son of An and Ki, the young God Enlil. I watched as he treated Lilith in a manner which caused me great disgust. I decided to make war against them, to teach them a great lesson but one of the other Gods betrayed me, and Marduk was sent to kill me. An, Ki, and Enlil had made the Heavens above us and the planets were held in the breath of my being, but this planet had not yet been born. When Marduk slayed me in my natural form, the Mighty Sea Dragon of the Heavens, Enlil parted the Heavens and made the Earth and the Moon. This is when he turned from my lovely sister, Lilith, and took the Goddess Ninlil for his wife. I have lived in disguise upon the Earth for many millennia. I have created chaos and despair to punish Enlil for his indiscretions against my beloved Lilith. I chose not to intercede until now. Not because I did not love my sister, but because I had to know in my heart that Lilith could do what must be done, without pity and without remorse."

Mes Lam Taea allowed the glamor of his Wargod persona to fade and stood before Tiamat as his natural state of Nergal which caused Tiamat to reach for his hand.

"I am glad the manner in which you were born caused you no strife. You are the perfect vision."

"What do mean the manner in which I was born?" Nergal asked.

"The rape of your mother, of course," Tiamat said coldly as she stared at Nergal. "Enlil pursued your mother for many years, but she was difficult. When Enlil tired of the chase, he captured Ninlil and raped her. For his transgression, Enlil was banished from Dilmun. He was sentenced to live here in Kur as his punishment. Ninlil loved him and followed him here. This is where you were born, along with Nanna and Ningirsu. Once their children were born, An and Ki saw he was a devoted father and loved Ninlil, so he was granted forgiveness. Enlil then returned to the Heavens to stand aside his father. This was when I gave to Lilith the serpent who could speak no lies in order to protect her from Enlil. I am surprised Enuggi never mentioned this to you."

Tiamat knew her revelation about Enlil's treatment of Nergal's mother, Ninlil, would incite within Nergal an uncontrollable anger that she could help unleash. Nergal's hatred toward his father's actions, both against his mother and Lilith, seethed from him as Nergal became Mes Lam Taea once more. He smashed his maces together causing sparks to fly, igniting a fire within Mes Lam Taea greater than Tiamat could hope for in her greatest dreams. His bellowing screams echoed through Kur causing the other Gods to fall to their knees and cover their ears.

"You lie!" Mes Lam Taea screamed.

Tiamat laid her hand on his forearm to draw into her some of the anger she had incited. A wave of euphoria passed through Tiamat as she drew the anger from Mes Lam Taea.

"Think, great God, to the day when you stood against Enlil in the War of the Heavens. Did not your mother stand with you against her husband? Why do you believe she did so? I can tell you with all faith, it was not only because of her love for you or how Enlil treated the other Gods. It was because Ninlil was still angry with him."

Mes Lam Taea's breathing was heavy as he listened to Tiamat speak against his father. He wanted to believe her words to be a lie, but Mes Lam Taea knew Tiamat spoke the truth. He looked toward the Heavens where his beloved Lilith was alone with Enlil and closed his eyes. He prayed she would have the fortitude to withstand Enlil and his deceptive ways.

"If he lays a hand upon her, I will kill him," Mes Lam Taea whispered as he returned his gaze toward Tiamat. He stared at her. Mes noticed how much of a resemblance there was between Tiamat and his Lilith, though Mes Lam Taea thought Tiamat's beauty was much darker than Lilith's.

"You love my sister very deeply. Come, let us speak alone away from the others," Tiamat whispered as she stood and reached for Mes Lam Taea's hand.

"When all the Gods have faded from memory, three shall remain. There must always be a balance between the worlds, light and dark, good and evil, a counterpart to the other for the humans to believe in. You will always live, though many years from now you will be viewed differently than how they see you now. Your Lilith, her legend will remain and her story will be told for centuries. Though I believe it will not always be told with honesty, Lilith's life will become the memory of things better left forgotten. Lilith will become a creature the humans will use to frighten their children into submission. They will not know what she truly is, the first vampire; a source so pure and clean her mere touch could kill them. I understand she has a child, one who she regards as her daughter and also a son."

"Set is a fine child who the Gods gave to Lilith as punishment against my father. Lilith allowed Set to offer himself to her and did not take him by force. He is but one of many who feel her blood coursing through their veins. Her daughter is different," Mes Lam Taea said as he walked alongside Tiamat through the caverns of Kur.

"This daughter, why is she different from Set?" Tiamat asked.

"Set was born from a mystical ceremony involving my Lilith's blood whereas her daughter, the vampire Ari, she carries not only Lilith's blood but also her host as do her five companions."

"Yet her daughter speaks with her not?"

"There is much bad blood between them. In time, the daughter will return, and once she does, then my Lilith shall return to me."

"You would wait for my sister no matter how much time passes? Do you love her that greatly?" Tiamat asked. Her question was like a double-edged sword. She awaited Mes Lam Taea's answer with baited breath. If she believed that Mes was lying to her, Tiamat would kill him without any consideration given.

"A year is like a day to we Gods, a century but a blink of an eye. I will wait for Lilith as long there is breath in this body. Be I Nergal, or be I Mes Lam Taea there is no difference in my heart toward her and the love I feel."

Tiamat was pleased at his words. She desired for Lilith to be treated the way she deserved, with respect.

"Come Mes, now let us make war."

"What do you have in mind, Tiamat?"

"I believe I shall begin with one of his favorite cities. One he came to love when he pursued my sister in Etruria. I shall destroy Pompeii."

Before Mes Lam Taea could respond, Tiamat had vanished. She appeared in the Hall of the Gods disguised as dove and flew into the hall, perching herself on one of the statues as she listened to Enlil and Lilith converse.

"Am I to believe you are remorseful Lilith? You, who bow to no man, would bow to me and ask forgiveness?" Enlil asked with sarcasm in his voice.

"I am not going to beg you Enlil. Either you accept my apology for my behavior or you do not. I have humbled myself before you, is that not enough?" Lilith asked.

"Given what has happened between us, the answer would be no."

Tiamat watched her sister closely as the anger within Lilith began to well. Lilith took a deep breath and pursed her lips slightly. There was no other Goddess who knew the art of seduction better than Lilith. Tiamat began to sing to distract Lilith from her angry thoughts.

"Have you so easily forgotten the acts that you have committed against me? Should we begin with Ninlil or would you prefer I began with Atumn and how you condoned his behavior toward me?"

"Lilith, I could not marry you. Our children would have been devastation and uncontrollable. You know that just as well as I."

"That does not excuse your behavior. It does not make me forgive you for allowing Atumn to take from me by force what I did not desire to give," Lilith paused and raised her eyes to meet Enlil's. "But then that is a trait he inherited from his creator."

Enlil flew into a rage and tossed the table between them to the side before he landed in front of Lilith. He raised his hand to strike her, and Lilith grabbed his arm.

"Strike me in anger and it will be the last time you strike another Enlil, this I promise you. Tell me, how much did it pleasure you to watch me suffer upon the Tree of Woe? Did it fill your heart with pride that you could diminish a woman to tears? Did you soar at the thought of the Shinkar vultures tearing the flesh from my body, piece by piece, as I lingered in the dessert under the searing sun? Did you make love to your wife each night after you came to me with the knowledge of supreme satisfaction over what you had done?"

Lilith continued to insult Enlil, badgering him until he was like a small child standing before her filled with guilt. Only then did Lilith rise from her chair. She stood over Enlil as she looked down at him.

"Perhaps now Enlil, you feel what I have felt and understand what sorrow and lament does to one's soul."

Lilith pulled the train of her dress into her hand and left Enlil alone, cowering on the floor like a small child as she returned to her room. Her plan was taking shape. It was slightly easier to manipulate Enlil than she hoped. Tiamat followed Lilith down the corridor into her room and transformed into her human form once Lilith closed the door.

"My sister, you have done well," Tiamat whispered as she wrapped her arms around Lilith. "Tonight I destroy Pompeii and Herculaneum. Then I shall destroy Oplontis and Stabiae in my wake. I shall call forth the fires of Vesuvius and burn the cities from the memory of man."

Tiamat kissed Lilith before she disappeared to unleash her destruction upon the unsuspecting city of Pompeii, then she would turn her attention toward Herculaneum.

As Tiamat appeared on the towering Mount Vesuvius above the town of Pompeii, she took great delight in what she was about to unleash upon the humans below her. Tiamat slowly raised her hands with her head down until her arms were stretched out straight at her shoulders. She turned her eyes toward the sky as her eyes became as black as night and Tiamat the Destroyer was unleashed.

Huge plumes of fiery ash and hot gases shot into the Heavens, twisting and turning as they pierced the clouds above her and blocked out the sun. Tiamat stood with her palms facing the Heavens as she held the plume of molten ash in place until she knew the precise moment was at hand. Tiamat swept her arms forward toward Pompeii and released the ash from her control. It raced toward the elite Roman town. Tiamat swooned in the aftermath of the release and took great pleasure as she watched the destruction unfold before her eyes.

The ash fell upon Pompeii with such an intense heat, it instantly withdrew all moisture from all it touched and essentially turned it stone. Mothers crouched to cover their children and were captured in the rush of molten ash. Husbands shielded their wives and lovers held each other in their final embrace. Tiamat watched with supreme satisfaction as the frail humans attempted to out-run the ash and make it to the seaport. They were overcome quickly, killed where they stood at the time of impact.

"Such a waste of a town born for supreme pleasures," Tiamat whispered as she returned to the top of Vesuvius and continued to unleash her fury.

By the end of the second day, Pompeii was not recognizable to the point that if one had not been there, the town simply did not exist. She then turned her attention toward Herculaneum and its destruction. Though Tiamat was slightly disheartened that many of the humans had taken the opportunity to escape Herculaneum during the ash storm that enveloped Pompeii, she still took delight in destroying the city and those who remained.

Tiamat returned to Kur and awaited the return of Lilith, her eyes still dark and foreboding as she sat in Ereskigal's throne. The other Gods were absent when Tiamat arrived. She contemplated where they had chosen to unleash their destruction and if she should join them. Instead, Tiamat returned to the Heavens above her to seek out Lilith. Tiamat this time took the guise of a golden eagle and landed on the end of Lilith's bed as she lay sleeping.

"Lilith, hear me. I have laid waste to Pompeii and Herculaneum while the other Gods incite war in lands far and wide. How fares your journey?" Tiamat asked.

It was not Lilith who lay before Tiamat on the bed of lavender. It was the trickster Enuki who desired to know the true intentions behind Lilith's visit to Enlil. He shifted into his natural state and lunged toward Tiamat, grabbing her tail feathers and pulling two of them free. Enuki fled from Lilith's room with the feathers held tightly in his hand as he called out to Enlil to warn him of Tiamat's arrival.

Tiamat swooped down upon Enuki with her powerful beak and tore out Enuki's tongue. When Enlil heard Enuki cry out, he appeared in the corridor to find Tiamat standing over Enuki. Her face was covered in blood. Tiamat spit Enuki's tongue out. It landed at Enlil's feet.

Enlil immediately dropped to his knees and lowered his head, afraid to look at Tiamat. The only Goddess who Enlil feared stood before him with an angry tone full of discord.

"Tiamat, you honor me with your presence."

Tiamat's laughter echoed through the corridor, raising the alarm to her presence. Lilith appeared behind her cautiously as she peered around Tiamat at Enlil, who still kept his gaze averted.

"Enlil your slick tongue will not sway me as it does the others. What have you done with my Lilith?" Tiamat demanded.

"She walks in the Garden of Dilmun upon the mountain. It was my gift to her."

"Gift? Why would you give my sister a gift? It surely must be plied with poison."

Enlil looked up at Tiamat while she stood over him. Tiamat realized Enlil was completely enamored with Lilith's presence. He had spent each waking moment lavishing her with gifts of great extravagance. Tiamat looked at her surroundings and the mounds of gifts. Tiamat smiled as she realized for the first time in Lilith's life it was her sister who played the cat and Enlil was the mouse.

"Tell me why do you give her these gifts?" Tiamat asked.

"Is it not obvious? I wish for her to forgive me," Enlil whispered.

Tiamat disappeared. She would leave Lilith to finish what she had begun. Lilith played a dangerous game. Tiamat knew she would have to believe it was one Lilith could win.

Lilith remained with Enlil for nearly forty years. She continued to rebuke Enlil's advances. Lilith kept her distance, always remaining close enough to touch yet far enough to escape.

There came a time when Lilith realized she could no longer continue the charade she played. The anger she carried in heart had softened. She contemplated telling Enlil the truth. One evening as Lilith sat across from Enlil at dinner, she decided to reveal to him what she had done.

"My ways with you have not been honest," Lilith whispered. Enlil looked at her as he waited her explanation. "I returned to the Heavens under false pretenses. I desired to teach you a lesson. I have learned a valuable lesson in doing so. I cannot use the emotions of another for my own personal gain. I am not like you, Enlil."

Enlil shifted his weight in his chair, leaning toward the right as he rested on the chair's arm.

"Enlighten me Lilith."

"I came under the guise of desiring your forgiveness. I wished for you to know the suffering you caused me. I wanted you to understand the impact your trickery, lies, and blatant manipulation had done to me over the years. Now that I have placed you in the same situation, I have not the heart to proceed."

Lilith stood from the table. She lowered her head as she turned to walk away from Enlil.

"Wait," Enlil called after Lilith. "I knew what you were doing from the moment I found you sleeping upon the stairs. I allowed you this moment of retribution as a peace offering for how I treated you. You were An and Ki's first born. It was never a matter of being able to love you Lilith. It was that I could not allow myself to do so. Look at what we have done to our children in our anger Lilith. Was it really worth the pain we caused the human race?"

Lilith walked toward the center of the dining table, pausing as she slid her hand across the fabric.

"If you knew my intentions then why did you not stop me?" Lilith asked.

"Much tragedy has transpired between us. We punished our children through our transgressions against each other. There must come a time for forgiveness. I will no longer pursue your children, the vampires. I will allow them their place among the humans. I would ask that you grant me one favor in return."

Lilith, knowing how deceitful Enlil was, did not trust his words. She knew he secretly conspired. Lilith decided to listen to his words so as not to anger Enlil.

"What is it you ask?"

"When your children are gone, that you would return to my son and be his wife. Agree to this and I shall never harm another one of your children."

"Why should I trust you?"

"All the while you stayed with me Lilith, I knew Tiamat shook the Earth below. I did not retaliate. I too have sorrow for the exchanges between us."

Lilith clenched her fist before she exhaled. "Give to me your solemn word you will not harm another one of my children, sworn upon the life of Ninlil, and I will agree. I will return to Nergal when the time comes."

"I give you my solemn word not only upon the life of my wife but also the lives of my children."

Lilith agreed with great reluctance. She knew Enlil could not be trusted. Lilith also knew that Enlil did not have the fortitude to kill his own wife and children. The vampire race would be safe for now.

Lilith's gown danced around her as she stood on the stairs to Heaven. If Enlil believed she would drop her lust for revenge, then he was a fool. Lilith had heard the one crucial word Enlil had said when he was speaking. He had said 'when' your children are gone.

Chapter Sixteen
Vengeance

Lilith appeared in Kur. She paced between Tiamat and Nergal. Her anger preceded her and was as expansive as the sea.

"He believes me to be a fool," Lilith screamed. Her screams reverberated throughout the crystalline cavern causing several stalagmites to crumble. "Enlil wants a truce between us. How can he be so naïve as to think that I would believe what he speaks? What arrogance! If war is what he desires then war is what I shall give him."

Tiamat approached her sister carefully. "I do not understand your question Lilith. Nearly all the Gods have fallen since Enlil's placement in the Heavens."

"Do they retain their powers?" Lilith asked.

"Yes. None of the Gods lost their power when they fell. Only their placement in the Heavens above was lost. What are you planning Lilith?"

"The armies of Persia still marches and is feared by many. Those who do not bend before them fall. The Saxons ready to march on Briton. Trajan readies for war in Rome. I will give them what they desire if they bow to me. I will make them Gods upon the Earth."

Destruction and devastation were two of the few pleasures Lilith embraced. If any of the humans were capable of providing Lilith pleasure, it was the Romans. They desired conquest, war, and were blood thirsty. Lilith would return to Rome. Her journey would not be one of diplomacy or to watch over her children. This one would be one of chaos with Tiamat at her side. She cared only for pain, destruction, and the misery she could unleash upon the human race.

Tiamat danced around Lilith as she thought about Parthia and Trajan. "Trajan will be a pleasurable conquest. He will obey my every will."

"You dream of pleasure when you should concentrate on war Tiamat." Lilith crossed her arms as she stared at Tiamat crossly.

"Why should I not find pleasure as I feast on their despair? How long have we stood in the shadows Lilith? How long have we waited our due sacrifice?" Tiamat asked as she circled Lilith. "What better way for chaos to exist is there?"

"I desire destruction. Enlil has forgotten how flawed his creatures are compared to my children. They argue over petty transgressions. Where I to make war against Enlil for each transgression he committed against me, the Heavens would have rained blood for the last six thousand years."

Lilith knew Enlil watched her from afar. He would not be so quick as to assume Lilith believed his words. There was too much treachery between them. Lilith seized one of the humans who attended Tiamat and ripped out his throat. Her eyes turned black as she turned them toward the Heavens. She released the man. He fell to the cavern floor, shrunken, and nearly mummified.

"That is strength. That is power. Their destinies are mine if I will it so. You cannot control their destinies through love. All they understand is force." Lilith screamed as she scanned the Heavens for Enlil. The humans in Tiamat's company fell at Lilith's feet. They clamored to touch her in the hopes they would escape her rage.

"Trajan makes war in our homeland. He desecrates all that was what was once sacred to us. Enlil favors the Mesopotamians. Perhaps, Tiamat, you should ensure Trajan lays them to waste."

Tiamat nearly swooned at Lilith's request. "Yes. Together we shall bind Trajan's will to ours."

Sara and Mes An Du were pleased with Lilith's decision. Only Nergal objected. He desired Lilith to remain in Kur and let go her vendetta. He sighed heavily realizing Lilith would not listen to reason. Lilith was bent on revenge regardless the cost.

Enlil sat upon Atlen in the hidden Garden of Dilmun. He could not understand Lilith's actions against him. Enlil was sincere in his apology to Lilith. He did feel remorse for his actions against her. He knew Lilith. Her anger was deep. It was not an issue she would let go easily.

Ki appeared next to her son when she sensed his lament. She was silent as she watched Enlil. Ki knew her son. Enlil was either deeply remorseful or plotting revenge. There were no in between areas with Enlil. He either loved or despised.

"For two thousand years you loved her until she was no longer enough for you. She did all that you asked. Lilith made the humans like her on our home planet at your insistence because she loved you. They destroyed our home Enlil. She followed you here, still loving you though your request had destroyed all that she loved. Then you scorned her by turning away from her. Is it so difficult for you to understand why Lilith behaves as she does?" Ki asked.

"Though I have made erroneous decisions, not one of them warrants her behavior. The humans here on Earth were never part of our quarrel yet she kills them. She does so only to punish me. When will her anger end?"

"You are not innocent in this Enlil. You placed Atumn within her reach knowing she would desire him. You gave her a Prince you knew could not withstand her touch. You sent Lucius to kill Ari. Lilith's children are all she has Enlil. They were created through her blood. The vampires who walk below us are all Lilith has that even compare to being her children. What if another were to conspire to kill your children such as Nergal or Nanna? Would you not then embrace the same rage Lilith has? By allowing Lucius the information to plot his revenge, you gave him the power to take from Lilith the only woman she ever believed to be her daughter. She cannot interfere in the nature of her own children, a fact you used to your advantage. Whatever she chooses to do Enlil, you will accept. Your actions alone begot the treatment you now receive."

Ki's words were harsh. She intended for them to be stern and cross. Enlil needed to understand this was the consequence of his actions.

"She will never forgive me then," Enlil whispered.

"Lilith has never learned forgiveness. There was no need for that emotion until she met you." Ki stood and left Enlil pondering her words in the shrouded mist of the Garden of Dilmun.

Enlil sat in quiet contemplation. There would be no soothing her. Lilith had listened closely to his words. She had caught the slip of his tongue. It was not meant to hurt her. It was an accident. Enlil knew what was coming, what would happen to all of Lilith's children, and he had not the heart to tell her. Tears streamed down his face as he watched Lilith and Tiamat woo Trajan into one of the bloodiest battles in history.

Lilith stood in the arid desert, reveling in the joy she had lost. The river was still cool, the shade of the palms still inviting, and the roses of her dead Prince still bloomed. How she had missed the Tigris river. Lilith looked high into the might palm that stood at the river's edge. She heard a voice familiar call to her.

"Hath you forgotten me, your friend who speaks no lies."

"Malach," Lilith whispered as she watched the dark green serpent wind his way down the trunk of the palm.

"I have not forgotten you old friend. Have you stayed here all this time?"

"I knew one day you would return, even if only for a little while."

Lilith reached up and stroked the snake as he pushed into her hand. She had missed him.

"You bring your sister. Will you make war now, Lilith of Sumeria?" Malach asked.

"I shall," Lilith replied calmly.

"Then I shall reveal what it is that you must know," Malach hissed as he wound his way around Lilith's shoulders.

Lilith spent the next two days with Malach as he spun the tale of what he knew was to come. By the time Tiamat found Lilith, she was exhausted from the near euphoria she felt.

"Go to Trajan, my lovely sister, love him and rise within him the desire for war," Lilith whispered in Tiamat's ear before she kissed her, flooding Tiamat with all the knowledge Lilith had learned.

Tiamat appeared in the center of Rome, her gown now brilliant white and glowing. Her fiery red hair was captivating. All the men in the street turned to see her, causing Tiamat to smile. She stopped a young suitor to one of the Roman Senators who was but fifteen years in age.

"Tell me, young one, were I to want an audience with Trajan, where would I find him?" The soft, nearly musical, tone of her voice commanded the young man to tell her all she desired.

"He is a creature of habit, my lady. Each day at precisely three in the afternoon, he visits the House of Mordia where he indulges in pleasures of the flesh."

Tiamat looked at the sun and its place on the horizon. She had an hour to find the House of Mordia and begin her game. As she walked through the streets, all eyes were upon her. Men bowed at her feet as she passed and women cried for the beauty she possessed. Tiamat arrived at the House of Mordia and laid her plan in place.

She leaned over the marble counter, drawing her finger along the arm of the young woman who awaited patrons.

"This day you shall lead Trajan to be with me, and in doing so, I will reward you beyond your wildest dreams."

Tiamat's breath was so intoxicating the young woman immediately nodded her head in agreement. She took Tiamat to the finest room in the house of pleasure. She closed the curtain as the ancient Goddess stepped inside and made herself ready for the man who would create her war. She brushed her hair, scenting it with fresh pressed jasmine and rosemary oil. Her skin she scented with lavender before rubbing olive oil on her skin. Tiamat reclined on the large, feather bed with only a finely woven sheet of cotton across her as she awaited Trajan.

Trajan was a young man, scarcely into his twenties and already an Emperor. He commanded respect with the manner he conducted himself. As he stepped through the beaded curtain, he expected to find his usual concubine awaiting him. Instead, he found a beauty beyond compare; a woman whose skin was soft and fair, whose hair was as red as the crimson sky, and whose lips sparkled like rubies.

"Come in, young Trajan, and find delight in the arms of an experienced woman," Tiamat whispered. Trajan was so enamored with her beauty he instantly obeyed. She tossed aside the sheet as he stepped into the room.

"Flesh is not the only pleasure I offer you," Tiamat whispered as she stood. She slowly removed Trajan's toga before kissing him. She slipped her tongue between his lips before pushing Trajan down on the bed beneath her.

Trajan, who had never been with a woman who could manipulate him in the manner Tiamat did, was instantly captivated by her wiles. She was tireless and eager in her love making until Trajan was defeated by her lust. Only then did Tiamat reveal to him what she desired.

"I have given you a night with a Goddess. What shall you give me in return?"

"Whatever you desire," Trajan whispered as he slid his hand down the sleek lines of her back.

"Even if I desire a conquered nation, would you make war for me?" Tiamat asked.

"I would make war for you and give to you any nation you desired."

"Good," Tiamat said as she turned onto her side. "Then we have an accord?"

Trajan nodded his head. He was now Tiamat's pawn and would do whatever she willed.

"I want you to conquer my homeland and give her back to me. I want you to make war against Mesopotamia."

Tiamat spent the next four hours with Trajan discussing military strategy and advancement. He left late the next morning to speak with his advisors. As part of their bargain, Tiamat traveled with Trajan to the land that was once her home. There she could continue to ply him with her sexuality and keep a firm grasp on the task at hand.

Days turned into months, months into years, until a decade had passed. Tiamat was pleased in her manipulation of Trajan and the deaths that occurred at the hands of the Centurions. The humans whom Enlil doted over and cared for above all other humans, the descendants of those he had first placed in the valley, fell like slaughtered sheep. It was only the beginning.

Blood soaked the sands of Lilith's old home as she watched the battles unfold daily. She took Malach to the crimson cavern in Kur and bade him to stay with her beloved where she knew he would be safe. The sound of clashing swords and chariots in battle as they crossed the sands filled Lilith with joy. Yet even in the happiness she felt, it still could not replace the sadness that lingered within her over the loss of her beloved Ari.

Lilith left the sands of Mesopotamia behind in search of her daughter. She found Ari had left Velch and traveled to a land far and strange; a land called Briton. From the shadows she watched her most perfect creation take her place as the Queen she was destined to become and cried for the child she had lost. In the sadness she felt, she still found hope when Morgaine fell ill that Ari would call to her. Instead she found only silence and the beckoning of the one who adored her as a mother, Liadan. Even in the darkness of what lay before her, Ari could not find forgiveness in her heart. Lilith retreated to her old home, the Ziggurat at Ur and cried for one hundred years. Enlil had bested her. He had taken from her the only one who mattered. He had turned her beloved Ari's heart dark toward her. It was a darkness that Lilith came to realize would only be healed by time.

The sands of time continued to shift, taking Lilith from one century to the next without a sense of direction or reason. She continued to incite war when she could, not because she wished to punish Enlil, but to control the population of the human race and to allow her vampire children to flourish. She continued to watch her beloved child, whom she held above all others, from the shadows as she awaited the day forgiveness would be granted.

Chapter Seventeen
The Gift of Lugal Erra

Lilith resided in her Ziggurat keeping a watchful eye over the children who were descended from her creations, praying the day would come that she could be with them once more. Lilith was one of the few Gods left remembered by man. She was grateful for those who still honored her, mostly women, who embraced her sense of free will and independence. Lugal Erra carried a deep sadness in his heart for Lilith. She had always had kind words and a caring nature toward him. He was unsure if her location could be found but pledged not to relinquish his search for her. The last place he suspected Lilith would spend her days was where he found her.

"Lilith of Sumeria, I have come to give you one last parting gift before I leave this world," Lugal announced as he stepped inside the inner sanctum of the Ziggurat. Lilith, who was wearied by the centuries, appeared before Lugal Erra nearly a former shell of herself.

"What has happened to you?" Lugal whispered as he reached to touch her face. Lilith had been so long removed from the world, his touch frightened her. She pulled away from him, nearly cowering in his presence.

"Come, we must find the Goddess I once knew whose touch took men to their knees and whose mere scent intoxicated them to near death."

Lugal offered Lilith his hand as she stood in the shadows. She was hesitant to accept his touch. She had watched from the shadows for so long that she had lost the ability to interact with the other Gods. She did not know they still existed. Lilith believed she was alone.

"You are far from alone. They call to us. Have you not heard their cries? There are many who awaken us now from our slumber, those who embrace the Old Gods and desire our gifts. Would you deny them the pleasure of knowing the only Goddess worthy of their attention?"

His words perplexed Lilith. It was difficult for her to comprehend how after nearly two thousand years of existing in the shadows they could long for the Gods of Old once more.

"This is not the reason I sought you Lilith. I have come to offer you one last gift before I leave this world."

Lilith stepped from the shadows. The color returned to her lips as she stepped into the light, resuming their brilliant shade of ruby. Her eyes glistened as she clung to each word Lugal Erra said.

"Leave this world, why would you leave this world?" Lilith asked. Lugal smiled as the red of her dress become more brilliant until it was the color of blood.

"There is little use for the plagues I once unleashed. This is why I have come before you. I should like to offer you one last plague against the humans as my parting gift. Let it be one final blow against the one who has caused you heartache."

His words were like music to which Lilith's heart soared. She felt renewed in a manner that had alluded her for many centuries. It was with baited breath she posed her next question.

"How will you enchant me, dear Lugal Erra?"

"A plague like none other before I shall unleash; where his beloved humans have congregated in great numbers. Come with me Lilith of Sumeria and revel in that which I shall bestow upon them in your honor."

She placed her hand in Lugal's without knowing where it was he would take her but with the knowledge the result would be glorious. The surroundings were unfamiliar to Lilith as they stood beside each other. Dense forests of cedar and oak surrounded them. The towering mountains in the distance were capped with snow. The air was crisp and cold against her skin as Lilith surveyed the forest around her. Lugal removed the camel-skin cloak he wore, wrapping it around Lilith's shoulders as she shivered in the cold.

"What is this place?" Lilith asked.

"They call this place Sicilia. Here it will begin."

They stood next to one another, watching the ships arrive in port. Lilith followed Lugal Erra as he walked the docks. He appeared to have a plan to which Lilith was not privy. Suddenly he stopped, boarded a ship, and returned with a small box. Lilith did not understand how a plain, wooden box would play into this great plan of Lugal's but she did not question him. She was quite certain his plan was a sound one. Lugal knelt before Lilith, opening the box and revealing its contents. Inside were two dozen rats. He picked them up one by one, kissing them and filling them with the Black Death. He set three of them free on the cobblestone street behind where they stood before taking one rat to each of the ships in the port and releasing it on board. Lilith was confused by his actions.

"Wait and allow it to reveal," Lugal whispered.

Lugal and Lilith walked the streets of Caffa awaiting the arrival of what he had unleashed. It was only a matter of days before the humans began to exhibit symptoms of the plague Lugal had unleashed. It began with uncontrolled coughing in some, huge lesions in others. The end result was the same; death. Those who developed the coughing sickness easily spread it to others. Death was imminent regardless, however those with the coughing sickness died in only two days. The humans who were unfortunate enough to have the Black Death which resulted in large boils and sores suffered greatly. They expelled large amounts of blood, both through the pores and coughing. They were wracked with pain and fevers. The doctors and priests of the day offered little help or comfort. They fled their fellow brethren in fear, giving Lilith great delight.

"Look at how his precious humans care for one another. They let the sick lie dying, burn their bodies once they are dead, and collect what wealth they can for their own. They are petty and insignificant, cruel and heartless, uneducated creatures that mean nothing," Lilith hissed as she walked among the dying as the wealthy and more affluent humans fled.

"Ah, yes, dear Lilith you speak the truth. Remember pestilence knows no bound be they rich or poor they will fall the same."

"I wonder if he watches from his precious throne above us. His love for them must be waning or he would have interceded."

"Perhaps, but it is possible he is so entertained by his current undertaking he knows not what has happened," Lugal replied as he looked at the ground by his feet, not wanting to look Lilith directly in the eye.

"What current undertaking?"

"He punishes those who do not revere him."

Lugal cringed knowing that Lilith would not be satisfied with his curt answer. Her eyes became black as the anger within her began to build.

"How does he punish them Lugal? Answer me truthfully for I will not tolerate any falsehoods."

"He allows those who hold power to extract confessions for what many of them have not done. They call it an Inquisition, though I do not know what it is they do other than torture them into submission."

Lilith's curiosity was aroused. As she gazed at Lugal, she began to realize it was not only the humans he treated in this manner, it was also her own children; the descendants born of Ari.

"What does he torture them for, Lugal?"

"They are tried for heresy and witchcraft." Lugal lowered his eyes once more. "And for consorting with the Prince of Darkness and his bride."

His words confused Lilith. The one who would be known as the Prince of Darkness was Drake, and he had not yet emerged nor taken that title. That would happen many years in the making.

"It is for worshipping you," Lugal whispered.

Lilith's demeanor changed instantly. She parted her lips, exposing her fangs as she clenched her fists.

"How dare he! Does Enlil believe I would not learn what he has done? Does he believe me to be so lost and complacent I would not come to their aid? He is still a fool!"

Lugal knew Lilith would become enraged when she learned the truth. It was part of the reason why he sought to unleash the Black Death upon the humans. It was his way of counterbalancing what Enlil now embraced and encouraged in his beloved humans. If he could kill as many as were faithful to Enlil as those he had taken from Lilith, then the odds would be balanced.

"I wish to see what it is he allows," Lilith demanded.

"I am not so sure that is a wise choice."

"Do not deny me what I must see with my own eyes, Lugal Erra, or you shall also feel my wrath."

Lugal bowed his head to Lilith before whispering, "As you wish."

He transported Lilith to the small province of Magdeburg; a town where few women were left alive. They kept there a house of torture as a reminder to be faithful and reverent. Lugal led Lilith inside. Upon seeing the machine which they used upon their brethren, Lilith placed her hand to her mouth and covered her lips in shock.

In the small house they had converted, they had built a rack upon which they stretched their victims until the ligaments in their body broke free, their joints, dislocated, and their bones broke. The horror of what she looked upon was nothing in comparison to what awaited her in the next room, a towering device that looked like a beautiful maiden. When Lilith opened the door, she wept when she realized it had been used to kill many of her children. The inside of the maiden was filled with iron spikes that were driven into the flesh with a wheel. Bleeding a vampire to death was one of the few ways a Hybrid could die. It was a painful experience that lasted for days.

"I wish to meet one of the men who completes this mission," Lilith said angrily. Lugal knew there would be no denying her what she requested. He took her to the house of the Chief Inquisitor and disappeared.

Lilith placed her hand on the latch and opened the door. As she stepped across the threshold, her appearance changed to that of a noble woman whose stature was a pious one. The Chief Inquisitor stood, offering his chair to her immediately.

"To what do I owe the honor of your company this day?" He asked.

"I am fearful of these days, great lord and beg your consul about the evil that surrounds me. I know not what to look for or who to trust in these dark days," Lilith lied.

"Child, you are a woman whose intentions are goodly and pious. There is much to beware. It pleases me as the servant of God that you would seek my guidance to avoid temptation. Those whose intentions are dark are many among us. Beware those who engage in sorcery."

"But how should I know this when they disguise themselves from us?" Lilith asked.

"A sorcerer or soothsayer whose manner engages them in the nature of spells, divination, or invocations will present themselves in a manner unknown to the untrained. If they are in connection with lost souls, thieves, marital discord, causing the land to become unfruitful, or take part in the collection of the parings of hair, nails, and other articles, they should be reported."

"How do I know if they are in league with darkness?" Lilith asked as she leaned closer to the Chief Inquisitor.

"They will herald Lilith as the first wife of man and bade her to grant them dark powers."

Lilith stood, allowing her glamor to fade. She seized the Chief Inquisitor by the throat, slamming him into the stone wall of the house behind him.

"And why is it that they should not worship me? Am I unworthy because I am woman? You would not be here had a woman not taken the seed of her husband into her. It is a decision I am sure she now regrets."

Lilith sank her fangs deep into the flesh of his neck. At first he felt the euphoria of Lilith's embrace then he was filled with agonizing pain as she drained his life from him. He strained and fought against Lilith as he kept his body pinned against the wall. His frailness beneath her only filled her with even more delight. It had been many centuries since Lilith had indulged in the closeness of ending another's life.

His withered, shrunken, body slipped from her hands as it fell to the floor. Lilith wiped his blood from her lips before leaving the small house. When her foot touched the cobblestone street in front of the house, it burst into flames. Lilith watched as the house burned to the ground before she embarked on finding those responsible and setting them aflame. When she rejoined Lugal Erra, Lilith had found all those who had falsely accused or led the Inquisitors to her children and killed them before she wept. Without a word, Lilith disappeared leaving Lugal Erra alone to watch the Black Death sweep across the land.

Chapter Eighteen
The Beginning of the End

Lilith wandered aimlessly without a sense of purpose for the next seven hundred years. Her heart could not find happiness. She relinquished herself to a life of sadness and lament. Though Nergal worried about her, he did not intervene. He had made a solemn promise to Lilith which he intended to keep. Nergal would not interfere in her undertakings. She would return when the time came.

Tiamat and the other Gods who had once graced the Heavens became the Gods of legend. Few worshipped them, even fewer knew their names. Only Lilith remained known but not as she desired, so in the shadows she remained as the ever vigilant Mother of the vampire race.

Her children grew strong and many. They lived in peace among the humans Lilith had once despised so greatly united by their Queen.

Many wars had been fought, mostly in the name of religion. Enlil remained untouched, now embraced as a new God, the sole God of a religion scarcely old enough to be considered a babe. He had achieved what he had desired so greatly; to be an exalted one loved by others. In the end, Lilith was alone. Her anger now long subsided, all she desired was to be with the one whom she loved above all others.

The Heavens above her had changed little. Her long fallen monument could still be seen on the planet she had once called her home. It was in many ways a sad testament to the life she had led and the life she desired to possess.

The advent of modern medicine led to the discovery of a miraculous kind in research. The ability to clone blood left her children with little to fret over. No longer did they have to seek out humans to drain the life sustaining blood from to continue their lives. Alistar Buscamante, the son of Drake and Ari, had made the startling discovery in the last part of twentieth century, though it would be nearly another twenty years before he would reveal the medical miracle to the rest of the world. Minor strife still occurred but it was nothing compared to the days of old when the clash of steel and blood soaked battlefields were the lyrics of Lilith's mournful song. She knew the days of her children were numbered.

In the looming sadness Lilith felt, she sought out the child who had brought her so much happiness. Liadan was overjoyed to see Lilith sitting upon the bench in her garden. Eire had changed little throughout the centuries and brought a sense of calmness to Lilith's heart with its gentle rolling hills and dense green fields.

"Mother," Liadan whispered.

Lilith smiled at the only daughter she had ever known. "My heart has grown sad without you. I should have been a better mother to you. I should not have allowed anger to cloud my vision and darken my heart. Forgive me, Liadan, I knew not what I did."

Liadan sat next to Lilith, taking her hand in hers. Her touch was colder than normal. Lilith knew her daughter was ill. She placed Liadan's head on her shoulder and held her tenderly.

"Do not apologize, mother. You did only what you could to keep your children safe. I love you as though you are my mother. Let nothing else matter," Liadan thought as Lilith held her. Lilith began to weep. Her tears fell from her cheeks onto Liadan's hair. Somehow Lilith knew it would not be enough to save her beloved daughter. The sickness that loomed inside Liadan was stronger than the magic Lilith possessed.

Liadan slept in Lilith's arms, exhausted from the sickness she now fought as Lilith wept uncontrollably. Her own obsession had prevented her from seeing the inevitable, from seeing what Enlil had warned her of so long ago. All her children were dying. All those that Lilith had loved during her life had withered and died, now too would die her children. The tears she cried that once brought life where now only tears that could not return those she loved to her. Deep in her heart, Lilith knew she had two years at best to care for and love Liadan.

Quinn readied a room for Lilith in the front corner of their cottage. Though he did not know who Lilith really was, he could sense her importance to his mother. He did not question either woman about their relationship. The sorrow between them was deep just as was their love for each other.

Lilith watched the grass sway in the early spring winds through the small window of her room. The world around Lilith had changed greatly in the last ten thousand years. The land of Liadan's birth provided her with a small sense of solitude. Eire was unchanged from the memories she held. She remembered the last time she had ventured to the Isle of Emerald and those she had known. Now only Quinn, his daughter Lenore, and Liadan remained of those she had once carried love for in her heart who heralded from the Emerald Isle. Her thoughts now were contemplative ones, filled with regret; regret over what she might have done differently if given the chance.

"Why so reflective Mother," Liadan asked as she entered her room. She sat next to her mother, resting her head against Lilith's shoulder. "What you did was done out of love to protect your children and secure their place in this world. Where would the vampire nation be without your intervention?"

"That credit lies not with me, my child, but with your daughter. It was their Queen who brought them to live among the humans not I."

"Without you, she never would have been. Enjoy the time we have now. Let go your heartbreak over the past. Now is the time for us," Liadan whispered as she closed her eyes.

Lilith held Liadan as she slept as Quinn entered the room. The pain Quinn held over his mother's condition was evident to even to those who could not feel the emotions of another. His eyes were filled with a deep sadness that even Lilith's touch could not heal. He lifted his mother from her arms, carrying Liadan to her room. Tears came to Lilith's eyes as she watched how tenderly Quinn cared for his mother. He was strong willed the same as Liadan with the soft, caring, and gentle ways of his father. Lilith faded from the shadows of the room before disappearing. She appeared in the garden where she awaited Quinn to join her by the arbor.

"It is time he came home to her," Lilith whispered as Quinn appeared at her side. Quinn was taken aback by her words. He had not seen his father in more years than he could remember. He believed Dagon was lost to the world of man.

"How will you find him when I was not able?"

Lilith glided effortlessly across the stone path of the garden to the well. She placed her hands on either side of Quinn's face, comforting him with her touch.

"He sleeps, my child, just as all the Gods of all do. I can return him to you. I will bring him home."

Lilith's eyes were a soft shade of lavender as she spoke. Her gown faded from black to a dark shade of purple with lavender swirls along the hem before she faded from Quinn's sight. She would need the help of one God, the only God who could awaken Dagon from his slumber. She would need the aid of the only God who had ever loved her selflessly and without intent.

She appeared in the crystal cavern deep within Kur. The beauty of the surroundings had not faded with time, they had become even more lovely.

"My love," Lilith whispered as her voice trembled.

Nergal emerged from deep with the cavern. Lilith's heart soared when she saw him appear. His beauty had not faded in her eyes. He wrapped his arms around her tenderly. "My Lilith," Nergal whispered. "Have you come back to me?"

"Soon, my love, soon we shall be together for all eternity. Now I come on the behalf of another. I must ask of you a favor."

Nergal knew if Lilith had traveled through the sixteen gates of ascension alone her journey was one of great importance.

"Liadan is dying. I must know if you can awaken Dagon from his slumber so that I might take him to her, to ease her suffering and give her peace in her final days."

What Lilith asked was no easy task. Dagon slept within the depths and would not be awoken easily. The suffering in Lilith's eyes as she gazed up at Nergal allowed him to see the disparity she felt.

"Wait for me," Nergal whispered.

Lilith walked the halls of the crystalline cave until she came to Nergal's bedchamber. She stared at the bed they had once shared fondly. Lilith laid down upon the bed, drawing the covers over her as she cried.

Two days passed. Nergal had not returned. Lilith began to fear he would not return, that Dagon was lost to them forever. The next day, Nergal appeared with Dagon at his side before the foot of the bed where Lilith lay sleeping.

"She punishes herself over what she had no control. How long has she been this way?" Dagon asked.

"I am at a loss to say for certain. I know it has been many years for I have felt her anguish. Yet I could do nothing as she would not allow my interference. She is distraught over not only the past but also what the future may bring. Her children are dying. There is nothing she can do."

Dagon sat on the edge of the bed and gently brushed Lilith's hair from her face. Lilith opened her eyes and began to cry.

"Come now, no tears. Together we shall make her days peaceful ones."

Dagon left Lilith and Nergal to say their good byes before their departure.

"I once told you I never wished to feel sorrow again. How will I care for her when I cannot even support myself in this overwhelming grief?"

"My beautiful love, you will have the strength to do so because of the love you have in your heart for her, just as you always have."

Nergal brushed the tears from her face, catching them in his hand before he close it tightly. "Cry no more my love. Know that in the end I will be waiting still."

Dagon appeared behind Lilith, smiling slightly at Nergal before he wrapped his arms around her and disappeared, leaving Nergal alone once more.

He was silent as they appeared before the small cottage of his wife. He had only been part of her life for a brief shining moment and then she was gone.

"What shall I say to her? It has been many moons, too many to count, since I saw her last."

Lilith stood before Dagon, placing her hands in the center of his chest. "You and you alone have been the only one to hold sway in her heart. She will care not what it is you say to her. Her only care will be that you are here, now, as her hours darken."

Liadan lay sleeping comfortably with Quinn tending to her when Dagon and Lilith entered her room. His love for her was just as strong as it was the first time he had laid eyes on her all those long years ago. His eyes filled with tears as he looked upon his son and his wife who now had reached the end of her days. Lilith took Quinn by the hand, leading him from the room to allow his father and mother the time they needed.

Dagon brushed her crimson hair behind her ear before he kissed her on her shoulder. Liadan smiled softly in her sleep but did not wake. He laid down next her for the first time since their children were small, remembering the love they once and still had in their hearts. When Liadan awoke, she found the only love she had ever known and ever wanted to know sleeping soundly at her side. She drew her finger along the muscles of his arm as she fondly remembered the moment she had become his. Dagon opened his eyes and they filled with tears.

"Do not cry, my love. I have shed enough tears for us both. My life has been a long one, filled with pleasures unimaginable and love so beautiful the Gods were filled with envy. Only the chosen ones will live for all eternity. It is not my time, it is hers."

"I have seen her in my dreams. She is the light of her kind, their hope, and their avatar. I wish I could have known her as I did Quinn. The memories I have of our time together are ones I shall always treasure. He grew into a fine man, one who should swell your heart with pride."

"I feel fortunate it was with you he was able to spend his life. It was difficult for her. Ari had within her a looming sense of not belonging. For that I feel responsible. She had a mother who was not her own whereas Quinn had his father. He had you. I know she would want to know you were here with us. Will you not call to her and let her know how much love you held for her as well?"

"I shall but now my only care is you, my beloved, and the time we have together."

During her lifetime, Liadan had loved only Dagon. There was no room in heart for another. There had been no man before him, and no man after him, who could compare in her eyes. He had been there at her beginning, the night when she completed her cycle to become a Blood God, and now he would be there when her time came to end. As darkness fell, Liadan and Dagan shared the love they had held in reserve for one another.

Quinn's silence was nearly deafening to Lilith as they sat under the arbor. Finally, Lilith could stand his silence no longer.

"Have you no words to say?'

"I do not know where to begin," Quinn replied.

"I have in the many lives I have lived learned to start with the truth. Anger only begets regret. Do not let your heart be angry, Quinn. There was no other who loved your mother more than him, no other who loved you and your sister more than he does."

"It is not a question of love nor is it a question of anger. It is a lingering sense of doubt, a sense of lingering reservations about how different our lives could have been if only he could have stayed."

"There is much you do not know about the days after your birth. Perhaps it is time you knew the truth."

Lilith spoke to Quinn until dawn broke. His mother had never shared with him the circumstances of his birth or his sister's. Though he knew about the prophecy and what it foretold, Quinn did not know the full story behind their births and what each of them was destined to become as time progressed. When Lilith finished speaking, Quinn understood what his mother had sacrificed to ensure they became what the prophecy foretold.

"It was not so much he did not love, it was he could not love. He knew that if he held you too close, your sister could not fulfill her destiny as Queen, that your mother would not have the strength to allow Ari to spread her wings. This is why he raised you alone. He sacrificed his love for your mother so that you could become the man you are now and so Ari could take her place as Queen. The pain in his heart was great, so great he retreated from this world rather than have to live without your mother and without her love."

As the sun rose over the rolling hills, Quinn had a faith he had not had in many years. Despite what he knew awaited them, he understood the circle their lives had completed and the happiness that could now be theirs in the fleeting moments that remained.

Chapter Ninteen
Death's Warm Embrace

Liadan had not yet succumbed to the Haven Virus when Quinn fell ill. Lilith knew the anger Ari carried deep within her heart had not diminished in the many centuries she embraced it. When Liadan announced to Dagon and Lilith she would send for Ari, Lilith faded into the shadows as she had done so many times before to give Ari her last moments with Quinn.

The crisp air of fall was about them. Quinn had returned home greatly weakened by watching Lenore die. He had done everything within his power to save her. In the end, it was not enough. Lenore St. Clair crumbled to ash in her father's arms. Quinn collected her ashes, returning them to their home so that she might be laid next to her mother. Lilith remembered the events of that day as Ari appeared in her brother's room, attempting to appear unaffected by what she knew was his pending death. Many she had loved had died, but none whose death would impact her as greatly as her brother's.

Ari sat next to Quinn, holding his hand as his breath became labored. Dagon appeared behind her, laying his hand upon her shoulder. She knew it was her father that stood with her as Quinn lay dying.

"Is there no magic you possess which can save him?" Ari asked.

"This, my child, is beyond the reach of the Gods. Our lives are a mystery at best; a circle that has no end yet must end in order for us to live once more."

"It pains me to see him suffer. It was he who brought me back from the brink of oblivion and yet here I sit unable to do the same. The Gods have been cruel to us in our lifetimes. When will the torment end? Is this the only way to be free of being their pawns?"

"Our destinies are not always revealed the way we desire or the way we would plan. Sometimes our strength comes in our darkest hour when we believe we have not the will to live yet we do so because it is our destiny. I know the sorrow you have held close to your heart. There was never a moment that I did not long to hold you in my arms and give you the blessings only a father can give. That was not my destiny Ari. My destiny was to guide Quinn so he could fulfill his destiny to resurrect you. We all must face the choices we have made. We can wish it was otherwise. In the end, all we can do is be grateful for the time we were given, for those we were allowed to love, and to know that it was not because we were pawns but were children of our destinies and not just a prophecy waiting to unfold. I loved you and your brother from the moment you took your first breath. No will of any God could have erased that feeling nor taken it from me, just as no one can take the love that you will always have in your heart for Quinn. That is the power of our own free will."

Lilith listened closely as Dagon spoke to Ari. His words were only slightly comforting to her as she held Quinn's hand. She closed her eyes at the sorrow Ari felt. It was the same darkness Lilith had held in her own heart many times, the loss of love. Together Ari and Quinn reminisced about the lives they had led.

"Do you remember the beauty of the Nile?" Quinn asked.

"I do, very fondly. I had wished we could have kept her as our home on many occasions. While it was a land of many painful memories, it was also a land rich in happy ones. I miss Ramses and many we grew to love there still."

"I miss the little mudbrick house," Quinn said and snickered slightly.

"How could you miss such a meager existence when you have a lovely home here in Eire?" Ari asked.

"There I was happy. There I had my family about me and my life was simple. There I had you."

Quinn closed his eyes, resting his head in Ari's lap as she stroked his hair. Her life had been a complicate one with the responsibility she held and had not allowed her the luxury of loving her brother the way she had wanted. He was a constant fixture in her life, yet they had spent little time together in comparison to the time she had spent with others. Quinn died as Ari held him. Her grief was infectious and spread through the other members of her family. Lilith wept in the shadows alone, unwilling to reveal her presence. It would only be a matter of days before Liadan would leave the land that had once been her home, leaving Dagon and Lilith alone to comfort each other in their grief.

After Liadan's death, Lilith left to pursue Enlil whom she felt was responsible for all that had happened to her children. She appeared on the stairs of the Heavens and awaited his arrival. She would wait until nearly two months before the alignment, an alignment greater than the one under which Ari and Quinn had been born before Enlil would grant her entrance. The doors to Heaven opened leaving Lilith no choice but to enter.

The Gods of old awaited her as she made her entrance to the Grand Hall of An. Ki, An, Inanna, and Nanna awaited her. Enlil sat at the head of the table in the hall, awaiting her arrival.

Ki rushed to her first born, wrapping her arms around her. Lilith closed her eyes at the touch of the one who had pulled her from the darkness and given her life. It had been many years since she felt an embrace filled with such love. Enlil stood, welcoming Lilith to come to his side.

"I have little to say to you Enlil. Why must you continue to punish me? Did we not once make a pact to let go this vendetta between us?"

"Lilith, it is not my will by which your children die. It is the will of the Universe around us. That which allowed their creation will also claim them."

"Yet it is my children alone who perish and not yours? When will my justice be served?" Lilith asked angrily.

"Their ways are not long, Lilith. Look at how they destroy the beauty of what surrounds them. Their planet is dying as a result of their own actions. It will reclaim them, then the humans will be no more," An replied as he gazed lovingly upon Lilith.

"All that I have loved, all that I have held dear in my heart, you have taken from me. Was it not enough I endured your treatment, or that I succumbed to the temptations you laid before me in the hopes of attaining love? Can you not in the last hours my children have left allow me the dignity of allowing one to live?"

The hall was silent as Lilith stood before them, bearing her soul in a manner none of them had before witnessed.

"But one shall live Lilith, the one whose heart mirrors yours the most, the one whose darkness balances her. She will survive for she is the balance. She is the light within the darkness and the darkness within the light. She always has been and will always be your most perfect creations. She is you Lilith in every aspect but one; for she possesses the compassion that eluded you for so much of your existence. She is now the source, the wellspring from which they all will spring," Inanna whispered.

"Stay with us Lilith until the planets have aligned then go to her. Let her understand why it was you have acted as you did so that she may understand her place now in the world and why you could not interfere." Ki smiled softly at Lilith, hoping she abide by her wishes. Lilith reluctantly agreed, praying that it was not another elaborate trap laid by Enlil.

Lilith watched from the Heavens as the last of those who were once embraced by Ari slipped into the arms of her beloved Nergal. She wept as Ari placed Uriah's body into the sarcophagus that had once been her prison.

"Got to her," Enlil whispered as he stood behind Lilith.

Lilith appeared on the stairs of the Ziggurat. Her perfume was so intoxicating the humans fell at her feet. It had been nearly ten thousand years since her feet had touched the sands of her beloved home in Sumeria. The landscape had been marred by many wars and held by ruthless men. Now her home was finally at peace. Those who lived there were the descendants of the humans whom she had once cared for in the valley near the Tigris and the Euphrates River. The treasures of Lilith's age and Enlil's children were being restored to their former glory.

She paused as she ascended the stairs, placing her hand on the griffins on either side. Freshly restored, their lapis and malachite inlays shone brightly in the rising sun. Red rhodochrosite had been used to replace the eyes. Lilith remembered the day Ashnan had placed the rubies in their eyes. The humans bowed to Lilith as she ascended the final stair, stepping inside her home for the final time.

The altar where she had separated her host for the six children to receive stood before her. They would be the only ones to receive the host of Lilith in her pure form as the first vampire. They were the only ones who could endure her gift and survive. She had followed them throughout the centuries, never interfering and allowing destiny to take its course. Now as Lilith stood before the altar, she wished she had interfered. "Perhaps if I had then it would not be as it as it is now," Lilith whispered as she placed her hand on the large slab of malachite that formed the altar. An altar where countless blood sacrifices were made to her that in the end, were not enough to save them.

The humans followed Lilith as she moved throughout the restored rooms of the Ziggurat until she came to the room that had once been her own. She placed her hand on the door next to hers, the door that had once led to Shiamat's chambers. Lilith closed her eyes are she remembered her dearest friend. She could hear her laughter ringing through the now silent halls. Shiamat had been the only one who had loved Lilith selflessly despite her flaws and who had cared for her until the very end.

"I miss you dear friend," Lilith whispered as she drew her hand away. She opened the door to what had once been her personal chambers wondering if the items she had once hidden their still remained.

Lilith drew her hand through the air and the torches ignited, illuminating the walls of her bedchamber. She stood before the wall where her bed once stood and pulled down on the iron sconce before pressing a sequenced series of stones upon the wall. A small passage opened into which Lilith disappeared. The treasures she had so carefully hidden, which had meaning only to her, still remained safe within the confines of where she had left them.

Lilith picked up the six chalices one by one carefully placing them into the chest that had been used to transport them to the Ziggurat when Ari and her companions had arrived. She picked up the ceremonial blade that she had used to draw her blood and held it tightly. Dagon appeared next to her, placing his hand on her shoulder.

"It is as they said. Our lives at best are a mystery but how wonderful it was to watch it unravel."

Lilith smiled at his words. Her life had come full circle. Her anger she had released; her love she could now embrace.

"She is here, waiting for you," Dagon whispered before he disappeared.

Lilith walked slowly along the corridor before appearing behind the altar that had been witness to the birth of Ari. She watched as Ari stood next to the sarcophagus. Her heart was full of sorrow. All she had loved had faded from this world. She had returned the one man, the only vampire, who had adored her above all others, who had never held a love as great as the one he held for her, to his home to be put to rest.

"My child, it has been so long since I have been able to lay my eyes upon you. You are still my most beautiful creation," Lilith whispered as she stepped out of the shadows behind the altar.

Lilith floated across the floor with her usual grace and sensuality. She drug her hand along the top of the altar before she leaned against the edge of the mighty stone. She snapped her fingers and the torches began to burn. Lilith's jet-black hair glistened in the light of the torches. Her ruby red lips parted as she began to smile. A gentle breeze blew through the Ziggurat and caused the opaque red gown she was wearing to ripple in the wind.

"I have waited two thousand years for you to forgive me. I now can understand the anguish and the pain you felt. All my children have left me, and I am now alone."

Ari watched in silence as tears began to roll across Lilith's perfect milky, white skin. The Goddess who was responsible for the entire vampire race, she who was the first vampire, now cried in front of her child. Ari walked toward her and felt the rapture of her love she felt for the only daughter she had ever had. Ari reached slowly toward Lilith's face, her hands trembling as she wiped the tears from her cheeks. Lilith closed her eyes at the touch of the one who bore her host. She was the only vampire other than Uriah who could withstand Lilith.

"Do not cry mother. I am here now," Ari whispered. "Tell me who you really are. I deserve to know the truth before I die."

Lilith looked toward the ceiling as though she wished to see the sky above her. Ari could feel how heavy the burden was that she carried alone for centuries. She was the only one left of her kind.

"I lived in the heavens once with the other Gods. I loved him above all others, but his love did not lie with me. His love lied with the humans he had created. They were such small and frail creatures, so insignificant to me. I never thought they would survive as long as they did. We created the heavens, the moon, and the Earth together. But my love alone was not enough for him, he turned away from me for them. I came here to care for them, his humans which he created in his image. I grew to love them as though they were my own children. But I was a Goddess, and they could not withstand my touch or my embrace for to love me was certain death, so I lived alone."

The sadness in her eyes as she spoke about the first man whom she ever loved was deep. Her sadness turned to anger and her eyes became like flames as she spoke of the injustice done to her.

"My only love sent to me a man, a Prince, for me to love. However, I did not want the Prince, I wanted Enlil to love me. I rebuked the advances of his Prince. In his anger at my defiant behavior, the Prince killed my lions. The rest of my legend you already know as the story of Lilitu written in cuneiform so long ago. I retreated to Atlen and there I stayed until six children were born under a rare astrological alignment. Six children who I knew could withstand my kiss and would become the children that I had never been able to bear. But even the alignment was not enough to protect them from the inevitable. My children all died, just the same as they had before."

"Lilith, what do you mean by before?" Ari asked.

"Your home is not my home, child. The ruins of my temple can be seen on a planet within your nighttime skies. We came here when all the people on our planet perished. Enlil wished to create his tiny race of humans once more. He thought this time we could be successful. Enlil did not know how his actions, and the consequences of his rejecting me, would end. I stood against him with his son when the War in Heaven began. I created the vampire race in my image to take the humans away from him, that was, until I found you. You are more like me than any other vampire. Within you Ari, lies the hope for our race. You are the perfect blend of mortal and vampire. This alone is why you have survived."

"I shall die too, eventually. Uriah has succumbed to the virus. I know that it will not be long for me to follow the same path. Even your blood that day was not enough to save him. I know it will not be enough to save me either," Ari said softly.

"But Uriah only sleeps, my sweet child. He will live not because of my blood alone, but because our blood will save him. Do you forget it was your blood which flowed into his heart as he lay bleeding, not mine? Do you not remember when I told you he was meant for you?"

Ari sighed deeply, leaning her head against Lilith's shoulder. The weight of over six thousand years seemed to fade away from her as Lilith held her in her arms. Ari had watched her entire family linger in pain for months before they died until it was only her and Uriah who had survived. Lilith placed her hand on Ari's stomach, smiling as she did so.

"His son will be beautiful," Lilith whispered.

In her grief, she had not realized she was caring Uriah's child; a son which would grow into a fine man and would be the mirror image of his father. Lilith took Ari's hand in hers and placed it over hers.

"Uriah's son will not be your only child," Lilith whispered.

She drew her hand through the air and showed them to Ari, six beautiful children who were spread out across the continents which had all been born at the exact moment of the 2012 alignment. Lilith evaporated into a mist and rematerialized by the Ziggurat doors.

"They will have the chance with you and Uriah that I could not give to you and the others. The choice now Ari, is up to you."

"But where shall you go now Lilith?"

"I will return to the only one who loved me as Lilith of Sumeria. I will return to the Hall of Nergal and pray his love for me still remains."

The depth of her pain was at last available for Ari to feel. For ten thousand years Lilith had lived a life of solitude and anger. She had only ever been able to embrace and feel the love of only one Immortal. She had forsaken him to oversee the creation of her children; the vampire race. At first she had created her children out of her rage toward Enlil, but later she created them out of love. The years which passed had allowed her to release her anger toward Enlil and his cruel treatment of her. Lilith prayed she could find the peace and the love she had desired but been denied throughout the centuries.

Lilith stood on the steps of the Ziggurat as the sun rose over the desert sand, creating sweeping shadows and contrasts against the horizon. The beauty of this sunrise was somehow different than the millions of sunrises she had watched before in her life. This was the first sunrise where he heart was not filled with anger or despair. This marked the beginning of a new day without heartbreak, without remorse, and with a sense of awareness she had never be able to possess. It marked the moment Lilith had longed for her entire life. She no longer needed Enlil. She was a now a Goddess who could embrace love without restraints. Lilith of Sumeria was whole.

Chapter Twenty
Solitude

Lilith walked the land that was once her home with a new sense of her importance. Her destiny had lied in the creation of one vampire, not thousands as she had once believed. They would live on through her creation. Lilith no longer had to worry. The War of the Heavens was now over. In the end, there were no definite victors, only victims. The war that had begun nearly ten thousand years before had come to a close. Only a few of the Gods were still honored or even remembered. They were the ones who were fortunate for the humans had not forgotten them, only misplaced them until they were once again needed.

Lilith knew she would live on in the memories of the humans not as the first primeval Goddess pulled from the darkness of the Universe, but as the dark creature who devoured children under the guise of night and who lured men into dangerous liaisons. She would be the night demon of their dreams, the succubus who destroyed the faith of men. It no longer mattered to her now. Lilith was finally free.

She traversed the desert until she found what she had been looking for; the Tree of Woe. It stood alone in the center of the desert the same as it had since the beginning of time. The Shinkar Vultures still sat perched on its massive, leafless limbs. Lilith closed her eyes as she placed her hand upon the trunk of the tree, remembering the humiliation she had endured and the pain she had suffered. She also remembered the kindness she received at the hands of Inanna and the touch of Set as he freed her from her bonds. Lilith stepped away from the tree as the wind danced around her. Her red gown clung to her frame as the wind intensified. The skies above her turned dark and formidable moments before lightning struck the tree. As the Tree of Woe stood before her burning, Lilith smiled. No other being would know the pain of crucifixion or suffering beneath the desert sun. Instead of satisfaction, Lilith felt a moment of sadness as she watched the tree burn. Another portion of her life had come to an end.

Lilith felt the wind brush softly against her skin as she walked toward the hidden gate to Kur. This time as she entered the sixteen gates of ascension her path would be an easy one. At each gate she left an article of importance until she reached the last gate. Instead of the gate attendant, Lilith found her beloved Malach awaiting her.

"To your home you have returned. With each step of your journey a lesson you learned until now you stand before me; a Goddess reborn whose burden has been lifted and whose radiance has returned. You are as beautiful as the day I first came to be in your care. Yet you are even more lovely as though a kindness has taken root in your heart. Have you mended that which hurt you so deeply?" Malach asked as he wound his way around Lilith's shoulders.

"Time has not been a friend to me, dear Malach, but instead a teacher. He has shown me that only I could heal the anger I held. I allowed my hatred to hold sway over me, when in the end, I was the only one who could set myself free."

Lilith paused before she opened the final gate to Kur.

"He waits for you just as he always has," Malach hissed before he slid from her shoulders and waited for her to follow. He led her deep within the crystalline cave to a room she had never seen, a room filled with his memories of her.

The chest that bore the Sumerian armor of the Samarra Six stood in the corner along with one of the suits of armor. The leather glistened in the soft light of the candles as Lilith looked around the room. The scimitars she had given to Nergal when he fought in the Immortal War stood crossed on the wall above the fireplace mantle. Folded across one of the chairs of the room were the remains of the dress Enlil had torn from her body when he crucified her on the Tree of Woe. As Lilith gazed at her surroundings, she realized there was a token from each moment of her life including her time in Velch.

"Do not be angry with me. It was the only means I had to have you near me," Nergal whispered as he entered the room.

"I am not angry with you my love. I find it endearing you cared so deeply. I am sorry I could not let go my hatred. How could I have been so blind as to not find my way back to you when it was you who loved me all along?"

"It was not yet time. You needed to find a way to heal and to make peace with her. Now is her time to care for them. I know you carry worry in your heart but know this is what she was destined for all along."

"Now can be the time of the new beginning, of their rebirth. They will be more than I foresaw so long ago. If only..." Nergal placed his finger to her lips before he kissed her, causing Lilith to forget what she was about to say.

"Stay with me Lilith and be my wife. I will love you above all others," Nergal thought as he held her tightly.

Lilith closed her eyes as she rested her head against Nergal's chest. She could still sense Ari. Somehow she knew her most beloved creation was about to embark on the greatest journey of her life and those she left behind in her image would be glorious.

Epilogue

Lilith stood watching the wind swept sand. One human had survived the Haven virus. She was an enigma, the one who had managed to survive. A curious blend of two beings, one being Lilith herself, the other being someone who had once been an age old enemy. The new breed of vampires had emerged at the hand of her beloved Ari and Uriah. Their place in the world was secured and they flourished. She was uncertain how Candace had survived until she considered something she hadn't before. "Van Helsing," Lilith whispered as the sky above darkened. "And so it begins."

To discover how Candace becomes part of the storyline as a descendant of Lilith of Sumeria and the great Van Helsing, purchase Vile Darkness by Kevin C. Davison.

Reference List of the Gods

An-Mesopotamian/Sumerian-the Supreme God who
     formed the cosmos with his wife Ki. He is
     known as the Bull of Heaven. Heaven and
     Earth were inseparable until the birth of his
     Son Enlil. Enlil then carried away the heavens
     after he split them in two.

Ashnan-Sumerian-the God of the Simug. Little is known
     about him except the Battle of Ashnan and Lahar,
     which mirrors the story of Cain and Abel nearly
     exactly.

Astarte-Assyrian/Hittite/Babylonian-Goddess of War
     and Destruction who later became a Mother
     Goddess and Goddess of Fertility.

Belet-Seri-Mesopotamian/Sumerian chthonic Underworld
     Goddess who recorded the names of the dead before
     entering the Underworld. Known as the Scribe of
     the Dead, to have your name written upon her list
     meant certain death.

Enuki-Mesopotamian/Sumerian. God of deceptions.
     Known as the trickster.

Enuggi-Mesopotamian/Sumerian-the throne bearer and
     attendant of Enlil.

Ereskigal-Mesopotamian/Sumerian. The Goddess who
     spins the thread that weaves the lives of man, and
     is the consort of Nergal. Similar to the Greek
     Goddess Persephone in some texts.

Erra-Mesopotamian/Babylonian/Akkadian-may originally
     have been theWar God Sara from Sumeria. Closely
     identified with the God Nergal, Erra is also the

God of raids, riots, and scorched earth and is also a
plague God.

Inanna-Mesopotamian/Sumerian-the paramount
Goddess of the Sumerian pantheon, born of the God
Nanna. She is a warrior Goddess but is also
concerned with the fertility of the natural world.
She is part of a triad involved in the primordial
battle between good and evil. Her sacred tree
was a golden apple tree which resided in the Garden
of Dilmun that held the knowledge of all the Gods.

Ki-Mesopotamian/Sumerian-the Supreme wife of An and
mother of Enlil. When Enlil split the heaven from
Earth, Enlil gave the Earth as a gift to her.

Lahar-Sumerian-the God of Herdsman and nomads.

Lilith-Mesopotamian/Sumerian-the original fertility
Goddess of the Sumerian people. She guarded
the Garden of Dilmun which resided on the great
Mountain Atlen. She cared for human kind but
was later named the Goddess of Desolation. She is
known by many different variations of her name
including Liluri, Lilitu, Lilari, and Lilnil. She
later was demonized and became part of the
creation myth to be the first wife of Atumn (Adam).

Lugal Irra-Mesopotamian/Sumerian- a counterpart of Mes
Lam Taea, the provider of plagues, known as the
Lord of Plagues.

Marilitu-Mesopotamian/Sumerian-six armed creatures
who were said to have grown from the blood of
Lilith when the Prince killed her Sacred Lions.
They were the guardians of humankind and helped
them to sow the land and reap the harvest after

Lilith taught humans agriculture.

Mes An Du-Sumerian/Babylonian/Akkadian-the bright and
  shining rays of the sun. He often blinded foes in
  battle.

Mes Lam Taea-Sumerian/Babylonian/Akkadian-the dark
  and aggressive aspect of Nergal when immersed
  in war.

Nergal-Sumerian/Babylonian-the son of Enlil and Ninlil.
  Husband of Ereskigal and God of War, Sudden
  Death, the Underworld, and Plagues. He
  is shown with a double edged mace-scimitar
  embellished with two lion heads

Ningirama-Sumerian-God of magic.

Ninlil-Mesopotamian/Sumerian-consort and wife of
  Enlil. Goddess of the Sky who is the mother
  of Nana the Moon God and Nergal the God of
  the Underworld.

Sara-Sumerian-God of War.

Sebitti-Mesopotamian/Babylonian/Akkadian-group of war
  Gods who fight beneath Erra/Sara. They are the
  lessor Children of An and are always with Erra/Sara
  in battle.

Set-Egyptian. God of Hostility and Violence. Also known
  as Seth or Setes. He is often linked to the Goddess
  Astarte in the Syrian pantheon who was the
  Goddess of the evening star, war, and sexual love.

Tiamat- Babylonian/Akkadian. The primordial Goddess of
  Creation and Chaos. It was said she was the Sea
  Dragon of the Heavens who was cleaved in two
  by Marduk to create Heaven and Earth. Later
  adapted by Sumerian pantheons.

Reference

Encyclopedia of the Gods, by Michael Jordan, a comprehensive collection of over 2500 deities.

www.en.wikipedia.org/wiki/Solomon

www.lilithgallery.com

Additional Works By Candace L. Bowser

<u>_The Origins Vampire Trilogy_</u>
Origins Blood in the Sand
Origins Reign of Blood
Origins The Blood Key

Kashmir

The Mirror

The Wolves of Dullahan

Mantis Pray for Death

Forthcoming Releases

Ascent of Darkness

Thirteen Pieces of Eight

About the Author...

Candace L. Bowser was born in Altoona, Pennsylvania and reared in Bedford County. Her love of horror was born at an early age. She credits her love of writing to the influence of both her parents, who encouraged her to read the great works of literature. Though she has a penchant for horror, she also writes in the genres of suspense, mystery, adventure, and paranormal.

Currently, Candace resides in Kansas City with her husband Todd of twenty-five years where she is working on a cyberpunk novel, Ascent of Darkness and a new vampire novel about the adventures of Florian Reinhardt entitled Thirteen Pieces of Eight.

2017919R00111

Printed in Great Britain
by Amazon.co.uk, Ltd.,
Marston Gate.